THE WRATH OF WINTER

THE WRATH OF WINTER

THE LEGENDS OF ANTICUUS NOVELLA

ROBIN WINCKLER

Published in the United States of America

Editors: Laine and Aria Nichols (avadel-ink.com)

Cover and Illustrations: Robin Winckler

ISBN: 979-8-9867747-2-5 (paperback), 979-8-9867747-1-8 (hardback)

First Edition: December 2023

10 9 8 7 6 5 4 3 2 1

The Wrath of Winter

"There is a myth in the elvish kingdom of a time long ago, when the wrath of winter came upon the land and the world turned to ice..."

— THE HISTORY OF CALISTIE, VOL. III

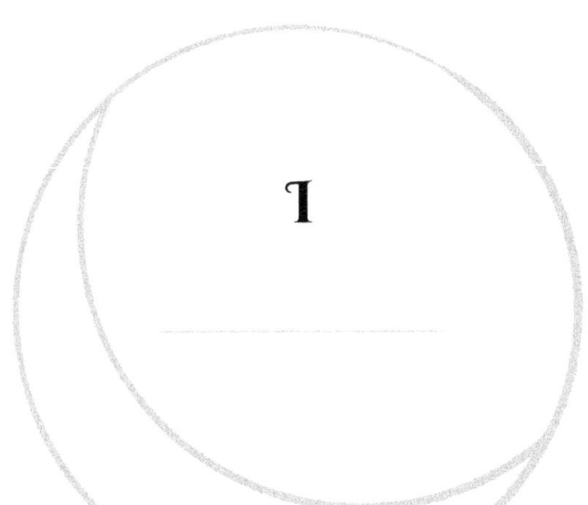

1

Tetsunah never imagined ice could be so cold. It shouldn't have come as a surprise, and yet it always did. Her entire body shrank back from its bitter touch; her breath caught in her throat, held there until her lungs began to ache. Raw cold chilled her to the bone until she was certain she would never be warm again—even if the sun consumed her and burned her flesh away.

Still, this feeling she imagined was nothing compared to the sickness that ate away at her people.

She cradled someone else's hand with blue-tipped fingers, its skin cracked and peeling from the relentless nip of the cold. Though Tetsunah held it steady in her grip, the hand couldn't stop trembling. It belonged to a young boy, barely older than eight years, small and fragile as he cradled his limbs close to his core to keep as much warmth in as possible. His gray eyes were wide as they studied her face, flitting across her expression nervously. Delicate coils of frost had already bloomed across his exposed cheeks, and when he exhaled through his tremors, his breath fogged in the air.

Still, Tetsunah dragged a smile to her face, pleasant and

warm like she always tried to be to hide the storm brewing inside her. "Can you feel when I do this?" She squeezed his hand.

The boy shook his head. "I–I can't feel anything," he said, words broken by shivers. "Just… *cold*. Lady Tetsunah, a-am I going to die?"

"Of course not." She leaned in and brushed his matted hair from his face, tucking it behind his elongated, pointed ears. They drooped to mirror the fear that creased his brow, tips red from the cold that clung to him like death. Pity pricked her heart. *I must stay calm.*

She took in a deep breath to clear her mind, inhaling slowly through her nose before exhaling through her mouth. A droplet of magic pulled from her chest and fell to the tip of her fingers, warming his skin as she let it flow into him. He breathed deeply and stilled, tremors ceasing. Gently, she eased him back against the pillow and pulled the quilted blanket up to his chin. "Get some rest. I'll be back to check on you after sunrise."

She left the room before he could respond and closed the door behind her with a sigh. It sealed the chill in the room, blocked out the lantern light that illuminated the boy's frightened expression, but it could not remove the image from her mind. In the flickering light, the shadows in his face were sharper, almost haunting. Leaning against the door, Tetsunah put her head in her hands, gritting her teeth against the tightness in her throat. *His skin is already hardening with frost. How many days does that leave for someone so fragile?*

"Lady Tetsunah?"

Tetsunah snapped upright, ears pricked. The boy's mother stood before her, wiping her hands on an apron. Her pale skin was turning red already, cracking to reveal veins of ice beneath it. She was sick, too.

Regret pulled sharply at Tetsunah's gut. It was harsher than pity and made her head throb at her temples. The mother's expectant look was suffocating, and she felt herself shrink beneath it. She fidgeted with her fingers, glancing down at her feet. "There's nothing more I can do for him at this stage," she murmured. "I can ease his suffering for a little while when I come by, but the ice has already made its way to his heart." Swallowing hard, she tensed her shoulders and finished with the same feeble words she always used in situations like this: "I'm sorry."

"Is there truly nothing else you can do?" The woman's retort broke with the beginnings of tears, her voice teetering on the edge of a sob. It was more than enough to cut Tetsunah to the heart. "How long does he have left?"

"A few days at most." Tetsunah squeezed her eyes shut, already imagining the sight of his body. Frost would cover his skin, tinting it blue beneath a sheet of white. His expression would be twisted in pain, frozen that way for eternity. When they buried him, she knew the town would weep for another soul lost to the frostbite plague. Their screams would echo in her nightmares, always following her, always haunting her.

She could do nothing but watch them fall one by one, plucked from her grasp by the unforgiving cold. All while the icy sickness avoided her, as if it were designed to force her to watch others suffer. She couldn't heal them, but she couldn't catch it and die either. There was no escape.

The mother's shoes tapped against the wood floors as she stalked toward Tetsunah. They carried her near enough that Tetsunah could see her olive green skirt swishing at the edge of her vision. Still, she refused to lift her head.

"Some goddess of spring you are," the woman choked out. Though her words were encased in venom, her touch was gentle as she pushed Tetsunah out of the way of the door. It swung open with a creak and slammed shut as the woman disappeared into the room.

Goddess of spring.

Tetsunah shoved away from the door, sparing a glance back. Its wooden face held no emotion, deceptively empty as if to say there was nothing wrong. However, she could hear the quiet crying from the other side—the sound of a mother telling her son the truth which Tetsunah could not speak. Nails dug into her palms as she clenched her fists. Turning sharply on her heels, she left without a goodbye, her cloak fluttering behind her.

I'm no goddess at all. Just a spirit, the embodiment of a season, and I am not the master of ice and snow.

As soon as she stepped outside the cabin, away from the warmth of the hearth, she was pricked by the chill in the air. Shivering, she wrapped her arms around herself, bundling her hands in her thick outer cloak, imagining the maroon fabric twined with gold threads to be a fire that would shield her. It did little by way of protection, but the thought eased her mind.

A sliver of light shone from the crescent moon, painting the village in a cool glow. The tiny moon hung back, nearly swallowed by the vast expanse of the night sky and buried behind its lustrous court of stars. Even with so little light, she knew the grass beneath her feet to be green. It whispered to her, laced with the magic deep within her. The breeze sang of spring as it brushed her cheek.

But a chill permeated the air, one that didn't belong in her evergreen village. The tune it carried sang of death, swirling around her with a foreign, haunting melody. Claws raked her skin, pressing icy tips beneath her flesh. Darkness was growing in the distance, a storm that rolled steadily toward her home, and it promised only more suffering. She gripped her cloak tighter and clenched her jaw. The sickness hung all around her, clinging to her, her land, and her people. Losing her grip on spring was the last thing she needed. *This has to stop.*

Tetsunah lifted her chin and strode away from the tiny cabin. Dirt and gravel scraped the soles of her boots, leading her down the road that spread out like branches from the trunk of a tree throughout the small town of Aire. At the late hour of the night, there was no one else wandering the streets, but she passed many windows alight with a candle inside. The curtains were drawn, but she could see shadows of figures against them: talking in hushed voices, coughing into their fists, warming themselves by the light of the fire. She looked away.

"There has to be an explanation for this," she muttered to herself as she walked, folding one arm over her chest as she cupped her chin in her hand with the other. Anything to keep her mind from wandering back to the boy's fear-filled eyes. "Maybe I've overlooked something. There has to be a way to fix this."

It had come on suddenly. The first unlucky ones fell victim to violent chills in the middle of summer, the warmest season, belonging to the spirit Deiah. Unable to recover, they died shortly after, their bodies consumed by ice that appeared out of nowhere. It came in waves after that, taking the lives of countless others. The more the frost sickness claimed, the colder the air became, as if winter itself had crept in early. Tetsunah prided herself on the ever-current warm climate surrounding the town of Aire—it was why so many flocked to live under her care. Now, it was destroyed by a force she couldn't understand or protect them from. Even worse, a massive storm was brewing in the distance, its dark clouds glistening with flecks of blue magic. Even from far away, she could see the ice raining down from it. She posted guards to keep watch over the storm. If it got too close, the sickness would be the least of her concerns.

All the signs pointed to winter and its spirit. If she could get ahold of Sefah, perhaps she could understand what was happening.

Before she knew it, the road had ended and she found herself standing on the front porch of her home. Swinging the door open, she tugged off her cloak and threw it on the first dining chair she passed. As she made her way toward the library, she kicked off her boots and left them in the entryway. Rows upon rows of crudely bound books greeted her, stuffed into the shelves with stacks of parchment and scrolls between them. Many were kissed with a broken seal, having been opened long ago in a similar nightly search for truth. She kept many records of medicines and illnesses, but none contained a hint of the frostbite sickness she was facing. She cracked open a dusty old spellbook, flipping through its pages for something—anything—that would answer the storm of questions whirling through her mind.

"No." She set the first book aside with a heavy thump. The second book slid easily off the shelf into her hands, but its pages stuck together when she tried to turn them. Frustration tightened her chest, warming her fingers with the rush of magic. She stacked the second book on top of the first; it was soon followed by a third. Before she knew it, her eyes were aching, heavy with sleep, and the stack of books at her feet came up to her waist.

Tears welled in her eyes and spilled over before she could rein them in. Sniffling, she gazed down at her hands. The tips of her fingers were alight with a soft pink glow, warmed by the constant flow of magic that coursed through her veins. They weren't blue and fragile, coated in ice that slowly worked its way to her heart. She was untouched by the sickness, spared from its wrath.

"But my magic can't cure it, nor can it protect others from it." Dropping her hands to her sides, she lifted her head. "So why am I left untouched?"

Her gaze snagged on the desk at the far end of the study. A small, ornate box sat on the surface of it, glittering in the moonlight that spilled through the window. Her heart fluttered as she raced toward it. *The amulet.*

When the sickness first began to appear, she rushed to find the little device and opened her connection to it. It bound her to the other spirits, granting her the ability to communicate with them over long distances. She went first to speak to Sefah, but found his side of the bond empty and cold. She tried and failed more times than she could recount but was always met with the same dead end. Bewildered and alone, she turned to her books and fought to solve things on her own power. Too many lives had been lost and she still held no answers. *He has to answer this time. He has to.*

Gently, she lifted the box from the desk, cradling it in her hands. She skimmed the side of it with her thumb, feeling the ridges of the gold swirls embossed along its body. The latch came open easily when she flicked it, and the lid opened silently.

Nestled safely against the crushed velvet lining lay an amulet no bigger than the palm of her hand. Gold encased its body, and it hummed as she lifted it. Four runes marked the face of it, each symbolizing one of the Seasonal Spirits. Her rune glowed a steady pink, pulsing with the rhythm of her heartbeat. Across from it was the warm amber glow of Xenah's rune. The rune of Deiah had gone dark some time ago, a sight which pulled sharply at her heartstrings, but her eyes didn't linger on it long. Instead, she was drawn to the mark across from it, enveloped in a pale blue light that fizzled in and out. Swirls of ice blossomed from the edges of the snowflake-like rune, crawling closer toward the center of the amulet. Light. Magic. *Life.* This time, he was there.

"Sefah," she breathed.

A shout from outside jolted her out of her reverie. Pocketing the amulet, Tetsunah raced out of the study and flung open the door. Cold night air rushed inside, and she shivered, her toes curling as it ripped at her feet. Still, she sucked in a sharp breath and pushed through the open doorway.

Two men stood outside, lanterns lit and surrounding them in a field of luminance. Their eyes were trained on something ahead; neither looked up when she approached.

"What is it?" she asked, following their gaze to the distant mountains far north of the town. The massive storm cloud was rolling toward them, engulfing the night sky in a blur of dark gray, flashing with streaks of pale blue. Goosebumps formed on Tetsunah's skin, the hair on the back of her neck standing on edge. Magic crackled in the air, bitter and icy.

"It's the storm. It's getting close," one man whispered. He took a step back, shaking his head. His eyes were wide with fear, pointed ears downturned and red with frostnip. "It must be Sefah—all of it. First, Lady Deiah turns up dead and now this?"

"We're being punished," the second added. "There's no other explanation."

Tetsunah chewed the inside of her cheek. The icy sickness, the growing winter storm, the flickering snow rune... She pressed a hand against the amulet tucked away in the pocket of her dress. It hummed faintly, pulsing against her touch. If she could have a moment of quiet, she could open the bond and try to contact Sefah again, but she didn't know how long that would take. If the storm swallowed Aire while she was away, she wouldn't be able to protect her people from whatever dangers lurked within. However, if she got ahold of him, he could stop the storm. *But if he doesn't answer like the last several times...*

"Lady Tetsunah?" the first man turned to her, voice quivering. "What do we do?"

"I'll go check it out," she said. "Return to your homes and stay there. I'll be back to advise us soon."

Both men nodded before hurrying away. When they were gone from her line of sight, Tetsunah returned inside, pulled her boots back on, and grabbed her cloak from the back of the chair. She checked the amulet again. It was still glowing with a faint blue light, the same as what flashed in the depths of the storm. Sucking in a sharp breath, she wrapped herself in her cloak and stepped out to brave the growing storm.

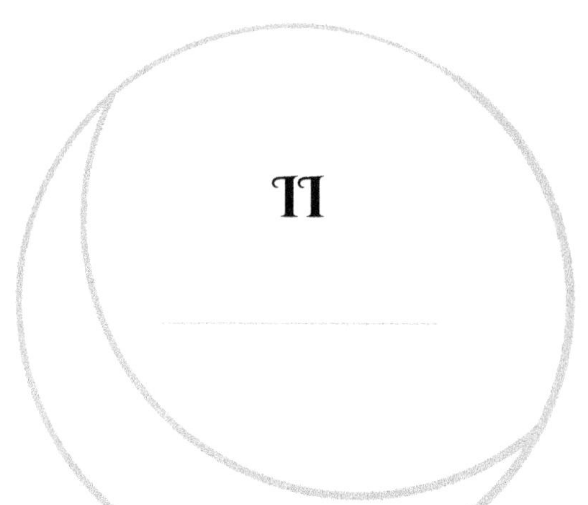

11

Far outside the town, Tetsunah had created a vast field of flowers that stretched all the way to the mountains in the distance. It was one of the first things she had made since her creation. She grew flowers of all kinds, shapes, sizes, and colors. It was her masterpiece, and she had proudly showed it off to the other three spirits. Dei had laughed then, frolicking freely among the flowers as their petals swirled in the wind around her. Xen watched with a peaceful expression, pride glistening in his golden-amber eyes. And Sefah... he smiled brightly. She still remembered his touch as he pulled her into an embrace, squeezing until she squealed with laughter. When she remembered Sefah, she thought only of his kindness. Though he was born of winter and lived only to wield it, he was the sun to her—shining brightly, always guiding her, always there to shed light and warmth on her path.

Now, she stood at the edge of the very same field of flowers. Cold winds ripped her plants from the soft soil, tearing the petals from their bodies and scattering them about. Frost marred the land like the claws of a savage beast. The ground wept—she could feel its cries beneath her feet. Overhead, the ice storm raged on, creeping closer and closer to Aire. It was only a matter of hours before it hit.

Fear and bewilderment warred inside her, fighting for control. With shaking hands, she reached for the amulet again. Sefah's rune still flickered wildly, nearly fully encased in ice. It crackled with magic when it touched her skin, pricking the pad of her thumb with tiny spikes of frost. *It doesn't make sense. How could someone so gentle turn to such destruction?* Dei's passing had made him restless—it startled all of them—but he hadn't shown signs of losing control. He had never been prone to such a fit.

Chunks of hail rained from the storm overhead. Tetsunah leaped back and swiped her hand across the air above her. A shimmering forcefield summoned around her, repelling the hail that dropped on top of her. Exhaustion pulled sharply at her chest, and she exhaled a deep sigh, breath clouded pink with the excess of her magic. Even this small display of power was enough to make her knees weak. She could do nothing against such a storm for long. The amulet hummed in the palm of her hand; she gripped it tighter.

She lingered for a moment longer, gaze stuck on the frozen field of flowers, now wilted, crushed, and ripped from their roots. Her throat constricted, and she forced herself to look away. *Focus, Tetsunah. The village. You need to inform the village.* There would be time to grieve what was lost, but the safety of her people had to come first.

Returning to the village seemed to take an eternity. The storm raced ahead of her, consuming even the sun's light as it began to peek out over the horizon. Showers of ice assaulted her, bouncing uselessly off her magic shield. Even that was beginning to crack as she ran, chest heaving and legs aching. Her mind buzzed with a constant string of panicked, anxiety-ridden thoughts; all she could do was run, feel the pounding of her feet against the ground and the harsh tug of power leaving her magic's reserves.

By the time she made it back to the spider-webbing branches that made up the roads, her vision had begun to flicker. It turned black at the edges. Her heartbeat roared in her ears as she stumbled down the path. She pressed a hand to the amulet, tucked safely away beneath her cloak. Wind whipped at her, raking her exposed face with icy claws and threatening to tear her feet out from under her.

"Tetsunah." A hand snagged her arm, jerking her to a stop. She gasped and swung around to face a pair of glittering brown eyes, darkened with concern. *Erix.* She recognized him almost immediately. The sight of him always made her stomach twist into uncomfortable knots. A similar shield to hers shimmered over his head, protecting him from the raging storm. But his magic was not enough to keep the frostbite plague at bay, as evident by the thin scar on the left side of his forehead, the skin blistered and blue around it.

His grip tightened, lips pressed into a thin line. "Are you okay?" he asked softly, barely perceptible over the howl of the winds. Tilting his chin down to better meet her eye, he raised his voice when he spoke again, "Talk to me. What's happening?"

"I need you to gather everyone and take them to the underground." Gently, she pried her arm free, cradling his hands in hers. She glanced down at their interlocked fingers, both red from the cold. His, though, were tinged a pale blue with the beginnings of frost. "It's not safe to stay here with that storm on the way. I'll meet you all there in a moment to explain."

He nodded, pointed ears twitching beneath his cinnamon-colored curls. When he slipped away, her chest ached at the loss of his warmth, but she forced herself to keep moving. She trudged against the winds, head bowed and arms wrapped around herself, and made her way back home. She slammed the door shut, leaning heavily against it to catch her breath.

In, out. In, out. When the world finally stopped spinning and her vision slowly began to settle back to normal, she slumped and slid to the floor. She fished the amulet from her pocket, brushing her finger across the snowflake rune. Closing her eyes, she pictured the amulet in her mind. The world around her faded away, swallowed by blackness that blanketed her vision. She gripped the amulet tighter and exhaled deeply; magic rolled from the tip of her tongue, opening her bond to the other spirits.

The amulet lay stretched out across the ground before her, each sigil a stage on which a figure should stand. Beneath her feet was her rune, the symbol of spring—a coiling blossom that glowed a faint pink, like her aura of magic. Deiah's corner lay dark, and Xenah's was alight in his amber glow. His form stood still, gaze fixed on something she could not see. Though the sight of him brought a wave of relief washing over her, she didn't come to speak with him. She turned away, questing toward the blue snowflake rune that fluttered in and out of light.

"Sefah?" she whispered. The tap of her boots echoed; the golden stage of the amulet's face seemed to stretch on forever. Breath fogged in front of her face; frost slicked the ground. The chill in the air grew stronger the closer she crept to Sefah's rune. She shuddered and pressed on. It was dark before, still as if he were simply absent. But now, something was off.

"Sefah, I know you're here," she called. "Your light's not dark yet; you can't be gone… not like Dei."

There should have been a figure—a faint ghost of Sefah's form wrapped in his light blue aura—standing in his corner of the amulet stage. Instead, Tetsunah found only ice and snow, flecks drifting lazily through the air. Spikes of ice split the polished gold of the amulet below her. It groaned as it cracked, spilling a clear blue liquid over the side. Tetsunah jumped back with a gasp, retreating back to her corner of the magic stage.

Sefah was gone just like the last time she had tried to reach out. However, this time, the season he lorded over was threatening to take control in his absence.

Her hold on the bond loosened; it slipped through her fingers like water as the black room cracked and shattered. The amulet toppled out from under her and sent her crashing back to reality. She awoke with a start, lungs heaving for air. Black spots danced in her vision, and her hands trembled, white-knuckled from gripping the amulet so tightly. It left the imprint of the four seasonal runes on her hand when she peeled it back. The snowflake rune burned her palm, skin red and aching. Sharp pain shot up her wrist. Tears blurred her vision. Lips quivering, she swallowed hard to keep back the painful sob that rose in her throat. *Sefah is missing. He's still gone. He lost control.*

She ducked her head as her tears spilled down her cheeks. "No," she reminded herself, voice trembling. The back of her hand swiped her tears away. "No. I have a duty. I can't stay here."

Even though the words flowed easily from her lips, her chest ached. When she thought of moving, the strength left her legs. It was an impossible task to stand, much less make her way to the tunnels, stand before her people, and confirm that the threat was in connection with Sefah. *Sefah,* whom she most admired, the one she looked up to, the one who always supported her. He had the kindest smile, a laugh like the gentle brush of the first snowfall.

Why would he abandon his duty to winter and let his power run rampant? More importantly, why would ice be eating away at the life of her people?

"I can't stay here," Tetsunah repeated in a whisper. Hesitantly, she pushed herself upright, her shoulder sliding against the door. The amulet hummed in the palm of her hand; she tucked it away again. Her hand throbbed with the painful reminder of what the amulet had shown her. *I need to go to my people.*

It took a moment for the world to stop spinning and for her legs to steady. As soon as they did, she braved the cold once more. Only a few minutes had passed since she had last been outside, but the temperature had dropped significantly since then. The wind had grown more wild, ripping through her long, braided hair and toying with her cloak and skirt. Hail pelted the roof of her porch, thudding heavily against the sturdy wood. She cast her shield once more, fingers buzzing as magic trickled through them.

The route to the underground was a fairly straight shot from her house to the outskirts of the village on the opposite side. When the town was first settling, she had created a system of tunnels for the people to take refuge in. At first, the intent was to use it to hide from the goddess Selini's people, the dragonborn—a violent race that had attacked the elves and humans many times in the past and always threatened to return again. She never imagined using the tunnels to hide from something created by one of her fellow spirits.

Marked by an old, weathered juniper tree, the entrance to the tunnels flashed into view. It yawned below her, stretched over the once-green and grassy field like a chasm. Her seal still held firm over the entrance, though the imprint of Erix's magic swirled around it like smoke. Holding her hand out in front of her, fingers splayed, she dropped through the seal and landed heavily on the ground below, knees bent to steady her. The seal passed over her with the warmth of the sun and a faint floral scent, shutting out the raging winter storm behind her. Relief whooshed out of her in a sigh, shoulders sagging as the tension fled her body.

"Took you long enough." Erix stood leaning against the wall leading into the tunnel system. Flecks of ice clung to his brown cloak, edges muddy from years of wear. He shoved away from the wall and unfolded his arms as he approached her, gaze softening. "What happened?"

"I tried to get ahold of Sefah again," she answered, holding her palm up for him to see. The snowflake rune marking still itched, as raw as the skin was red.

Sympathy lit up his brown eyes as he took her hand in his, gently skimming his fingers over the wound. "The amulet rejected you?"

"He's gone, but it wasn't like the other times. Winter is out of control. I think… I think that's why all of this is happening."

"Gone?" Erix's brow furrowed. "Oh, Tet—"

"Missing," she quickly corrected. Retracting her hand from his grip, she maneuvered past him. "I need to tell everyone I must leave. I have to find him and figure out why this is happening now. He has a right to be absent at times, but I can't stand by while winter runs rampant. Something must have happened to him."

"Leave? Hold on, Tetsunah." He grabbed her arm and pulled her to a stop. When she spun to face him, the look in his eyes was serious. "You're not planning to go alone, are you?"

"I have to," she murmured. She dragged her gaze away, her chest tight. "It's my responsibility not only as a Seasonal Spirit and the leader of Aire, but also as his friend. I'm worried, Erix. I don't understand why this is happening."

His hand on her arm slowly pulled away. "Then at least let me go with you."

Tetsunah shook her head, lifting her eyes to meet his again. "I need you here. The people need someone to look up to while I'm gone; I need to leave them in the hands of someone I trust."

Hesitation darkened his expression, lips pursed as he looked away. Finally, he took a deep breath. "Okay," he answered in a soft whisper. "If that's what you need, I will stay."

With a halfhearted smile, she made her way down the tunnel again.

Erix hurried behind her as she walked, their footsteps echoing as the packed dirt ground turned to rock. The smooth stone walls of the tunnel opened up into a large room that stretched farther than her eyes could see in the dim light. The ceiling was high overhead, the walls too far for her to reach on either side, and yet the room still felt too small. Everyone in the town had been gathered there already. Many still looked exhausted from being woken, their clothes wrinkled and their hair unbrushed and loose. They all raised their heads when Tetsunah entered the room. Sickness permeated the air, cold and biting as it brushed against Tetsunah's skin. There was only so much her seal could keep out, and the frostbite disease was not one of those things. Whispers and murmurs drifted through the air; Tetsunah began to fidget with her skirts. Anxiety crackled in her chest. She took a deep breath and cleared her throat.

"Everyone, please allow me to have your attention for a moment," she said, raising her voice so that it carried throughout the massive room. It didn't take long for the whispers to fall silent. Her heart thudded against her ribcage. "A–as you know, our people have been victims of the frostbite sickness for several moons now. The season of Sefah's winter has come and gone, yet the cold remains in my domain of spring. And now, an ice storm has come to ravage our town. My power is not enough to divert it, stop it, or be rid of it entirely. This is why I asked Erix to evacuate everyone to the tunnels. It's not ideal, and I know it's not the most comfortable, b–but you will be safe and warm here. Please understand—"

"What's your plan?" a woman's voice bit back. The mother from before shoved her way to the front of the crowd, eyes swollen and red from crying, her pointed ears flattened back. Her eyes flashed in the low torchlight. "We can't hide out here forever, and there's no telling how long that storm will go on."

Erix stepped forward, mouth open in a retort, but Tetsunah stopped him by raising her hand. *Calm. Deep breaths.* She lifted her chin. "I am leaving Aire for the time being. I tried to contact

Sefah, the spirit of winter, but found his bond empty and void. I believe it is his absence that has caused this strange disturbance. It's different from when Deiah died—summer settled on its own without her. There's something wrong. I must find him if we hope to have a chance at getting through this."

The woman bristled. "How do you know he's missing and not angry with us? The winter spirit has always been the most bitter; is this not simply the consequences of his wrath?" she spat. "You'd only be leaving us here to wait until the sickness claims us all. You're a coward; you can't face your failure here any longer."

Murmurs of agreement broke out among the crowd. Many turned to their neighbor, whispering in their ear as they cast scornful looks at her. Their words were lost among the hum of chatter, but Tetsunah was drowning in them anyway. Her lungs seized, eyes pricked with tears. Fingers pulled and twisted her patterned skirts, desperately working to distract her from the growing unrest. *Coward, failure, incapable, unreliable, weak.*

"Yes, I am afraid," she snapped back, silencing the mocking lull of her mind. Her voice wavered, but she managed to project it above the noise, reigning in the crowd once more. It startled the woman at the front and many others who were intent on cutting her open with the daggers they glared in her direction. All had skin split by ice, red with cold or blue with the imminence of death. They were the ones she couldn't help anymore; she owed them the world and a thousand apologies, yet all she could offer was a small shard of hope.

"I am afraid," she said again, more firmly this time. "Afraid of what might have happened to my friend, afraid of what the consequences have wrought on all of you, afraid of the truth I might find. But I'm asking all of you to trust me. I will uncover the truth of what has happened, and I will find a way to fix this. All I ask of you is that you stay here, lay low, and help each other while you can." Turning to Erix, she held out her hands for his.

He studied her face, uncertainty curling in his gaze. He masked it well with a smile as warm as the sun and stepped up to place his hands in hers, gentle as always. She squeezed his fingers, opening the reserves of her magic. It trickled down to her hands, passing from her to him. A faint pink glow settled in his skin, twining with his own power as hers sank into him. Breathing deeply, she released him and turned to the crowd again.

"I'm appointing Erix as the head in my place," she said. "I have gifted some of my magic to him so that he can tend to you in my place and uphold the seal while I'm gone. Trust him and do as he says. I will return shortly."

When she finished this time, no one said a word. It was a begrudging silence, one that did not settle the growing unease in her chest, but she let it go and turned to Erix one last time. He offered another smile, one that reached his eyes this time.

"Good luck," he said.

"Take care of yourself as well." She brushed a hand across the scar on his forehead; it was cold to the touch, though the rest of his skin remained warm. "I'm counting on you."

"I know."

She didn't give him the chance to say anything else. With one final glance at her people, still watching and waiting, she left the room and returned to the sealed entryway. Beyond its shimmering pink runes lay the storm—the full wrath of winter —and somewhere out there, the truth of Sefah's disappearance and his loss of control. She only had to find it.

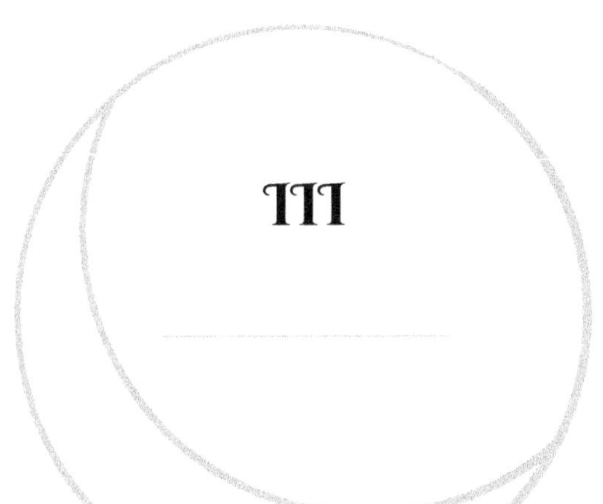

III

Once, when Tetsunah spoke with Sefah, he admitted he was weary of being looked on with fear by everyone he passed. Exhausted, he claimed he wanted to settle down and live in peace, where he could carry out his duty without worrying that he was frightening someone. It didn't stop whispers from carrying; elves and humans alike knew well of Sefah and circulated rumors that he was only a step from evil, always teetering on the edge of unleashing icy wrath on the world. It pained Tetsunah to see the sadness in his face when he heard such things. *"I just want to protect our people,"* he said once. *"I want to fulfill my duty as the Being taught me to. I don't want to punish or terrify mortals."*

When news of Deiah's death spread, he became distant and quiet. Still, Tet couldn't imagine that even grief would push him so far from his morals, but the plague fell not long after the spirit of summer passed. It was harder to deny with the evidence she had. She could only cling desperately to the Sefah she knew and hope he hadn't fallen away.

In search of peace, he had settled down in the far north, where he was surrounded by nothing but snow and mountains.

It was on the outskirts of the Calistian kingdom's capital city, where he and his family lived largely undisturbed by the outside world. That was years ago, and she hadn't been in quite some time, but it was a start.

Traveling north took her through the heart of the storm. If she didn't know better, she would have assumed she was journeying through an arctic wasteland rather than what had once been her fields and plains. The ground was slick with ice and snow, cold even through the thick soles of her boots. Dark clouds swallowed up the sun, stranding her in a foggy darkness despite it not being later than mid-afternoon. Wind and sleet slammed against her; they seemed to be working together with the sky to lower her visibility even more.

As much as possible, she summoned her magic to teleport herself short distances forward. Unable to pinpoint her exact location in the storm, she could only go so far each time. Still, it allowed her to cover more ground than walking would have, but each spell left her gasping for air and struggling to stand. It wouldn't have been easy at full power, but with half of her magic in Erix's hands, she could feel her strength beginning to give out. At the twelfth warp, she collapsed into the thick snow, glancing back to find she could no longer see the town of Aire. Only the fog of the stormy winds whirled around her.

Her whole body trembled uncontrollably, her vision tunneling until she could only see a pinprick of white. A throbbing headache split her skull. Bile wrenched from her mouth before she could stop herself, scraping the back of her throat and coating her tongue in a sour taste, twinged with the iron tang of blood. She curled her fingers against her palm, balling up a fistful of snow. The cold snapped at the snowflake-shaped burn in her hand. *Move. You can't stay here.*

The thought slurred into a meaningless thread, slipping through her fingers like water. Darkness consumed her vision, and the ringing in her ears cut off abruptly.

———

*M*AGIC *IS A FICKLE THING.*

Sefah was a master of the warp spell. He would always come and go as he pleased, phasing in and out in a flurry of snowflakes and azure sparks. He was especially talented at crossing long distances, even when he couldn't see the other location directly. He could just picture it in his mind and go there. Latching onto others' auras and teleporting to them was one of his specialties. He claimed it was a special gift, made just for him since his eyesight had always been poor.

In the early days, he would appear at the beginning of spring to help Tetsunah usher it in. *"Take it slow,"* he would say. *"Don't rush. Your magic will answer you when it believes you're ready. You'll get the hang of it, I promise."*

Tetsunah didn't have the kind of power he did. Her pool of magic was small, easily drained and slow to regenerate. She was the weakest among the four of them for a reason.

"Don't push yourself," Sefah would say, concern swimming in his brilliant blue eyes. The snowflake rune in the pupil of his left eye glowed constantly, illuminated by a bright, white light. He said it made it difficult for him to see, yet he seemed to be the only one who truly saw *her* at times. *"There are consequences for using up all of your magic reserves, Tet. Teleportation is not exactly what I would consider a viable reason to throw your life away."*

Why would she recall something like this? She couldn't remember. The memory drifted by, and she was consumed by darkness once more.

"Te…" a faint voice called out, small and far away. Something seized her wrist. "Tetsu…"

Sefah. Beneath the heavy fog smothering her mind, a glimmer of hope lit inside her. *You're there, aren't you?*

"Tetsunah," the voice answered, clearer this time. It took form as an elegant female voice with the lull of a Draconic

23

accent, noticeable for the way it rolled the syllables of her name together. A warm cloth settled on her forehead. "Stay with me. Koen, fetch me another blanket—and quickly."

A woman? Tetsunah shifted, weakly lifting a hand. It quickly fell back to her side, pinned by a heavy quilt that lay stretched over her. With a groan, she rolled her head to the side. It took several seconds to force her eyes open. The room spun, blurred and blackened at the edges of her vision, but she could faintly make out a face in front of her.

The woman smiled—or so Tetsunah assumed. Her fingers were warm when they pressed against Tetsunah's cheeks. "Lie still," she instructed. "You need to recover your strength."

Her voice was familiar, though only barely. A name rose to the tip of Tetsunah's tongue, and she frowned; it was there, but just out of reach. Slowly, her vision refocused, and she studied the woman's face more closely. Cropped black curls spilled over her shoulders, framing her cheekbones in elegant waves. Silver tinsel was woven into her hair; it glittered like starlight against her curls. Her eyes were a pale blue like glass, striking against the warm olive tone of her skin. Silver scales dotted her cheeks and nose, paired with two horns that curved out from under her hair. Her ears were pointed, though small like that of a dragonborn rather than an elf. *A dragonborn. One of Selini's people.* Still, the sight of her only brought calm washing over Tetsunah's mind.

"Kamari," she croaked, throat dry like sandpaper. The sour taste of bile still lingered on her tongue, and her limbs were heavy, trembling with exhaustion. And yet, relief built up in her chest. She sighed and sank back against her pillow.

Kamari smiled kindly, as beautiful and radiant as ever. She was the moon, and Tetsunah was only a star, small and insignificant compared to her silver glow. But there was no one Tetsunah would rather find herself with.

If there was anyone who was bound to know something about what had happened to Sefah, it was his wife.

Slowly, the tension ebbed from Tetsunah's muscles, allowing her to relax into the plush cushions. Warmth penetrated the cold that gripped her and quickly soothed her. She swept her gaze around the room, taking in the sturdy wood panels. A fire crackled in the hearth at the other end of the room, surrounded by stone and packed dirt. An open doorway led out into a hall that revealed another set of rooms beyond. Faint memories tickled the back of Tetsunah's mind. *Sefah's home.*

"Not that you aren't welcome here anytime you wish to visit, but..." Kamari sighed, her smile fading. She pinned Tetsunah beneath a pointed stare, a look that pierced straight through her and stripped her of her walls. "What happened, Tetsunah? How did you end up like..." She paused to gesture at Tetsunah, her nose wrinkling. "*This?*"

"My people." Tetsunah started to sit upright again, only to be stopped by Kamari's hand on her shoulder. She allowed the dragonborn woman to push her back down again, but it didn't stop the feeling of helplessness that pooled in the pit of her stomach. "My people are dying. Ice is consuming them from the inside out. It started back in summer and has only grown worse—and now, there's a huge winter storm rolling through and raining chunks of ice larger than my fist. It's destroying lands and—and I can't bring in spring this way. Kamari, where is Sefah?"

She visibly stiffened and darted her gaze away, twisting the gold band around her ring finger. "I–I..."

"Mama, I have the blanket," a small voice interrupted. A little boy emerged from the doorway, a thick quilt in his arms that almost swallowed him whole. He approached quietly, footsteps as light as a mouse skittering through the fields. When he came to Kamari's side, he held out the quilt to her, silver eyes flicking to Tetsunah before he quickly looked away again.

"Thank you, Koen. Why don't you go play with your sisters for a while?" Kamari accepted the quilt, feigning another smile. She kissed his cheek—his skin a deep bronze like Sefah's—and ruffled his coal-black curls. However, his gaze never left Tetsunah; there was intelligence swirling in the depths of his eyes, marking him as a young adolescent despite his small frame. He was old enough to know something wasn't right, but he obeyed nonetheless and left.

Kamari sat perfectly straight until he was gone. The moment he left the room, she exhaled a long sigh as if she had been holding her breath. "Let's get you cleaned up and fed first. Then we'll talk. I had Meliv draw up a hot bath for you. You'll feel better after." She rose to stand.

"Kamari, please." Tetsunah jerked her arm out from under the blankets and grabbed Kamari's hand. "Talk to me first. What happened?"

When the woman turned to her again, she noticed the lines of exhaustion etched into her face. Her pale eyes dulled, darkened by whatever weight had fallen onto her shoulders. Slowly, she sank back into her seat and began to fiddle with her ring again. "I was hoping you would know," she murmured, lowering her head. A curtain of black curls fell in her face, the silver tinsel in her locks glistening in the firelight. "He disappeared several weeks ago. I haven't heard anything from him at all. I went to the Aurora Range to look for him, but I couldn't even find a trace. It's like he's just… *gone*."

"Gone," Tetsunah echoed. A shiver trailed cold fingers down her spine. She chewed her lip as she carefully eased herself upright. As much as she wanted to say something encouraging or to try to comfort Kamari, the words wouldn't come. All she could think of was the fact that Sefah was *gone*, but he was the only one who could wrangle the encroaching wrath of winter. He was the most powerful of the four Spirits; he couldn't be *gone*.

"You have that amulet, right?" Kamari asked. "What did it tell you?"

"The same thing." Tetsunah reached into her cloak and pulled out the amulet, offering it to Kamari. Sefah's rune still lay buried in ice, flickering like a dying flame. "When I tapped into it, he wasn't there at all, but it doesn't feel empty like Deiah's side. It feels... blocked? It was different from the other times I tried to contact him. Even within the amulet, winter is running wild." She shifted her grip on the amulet to reveal the burn on her hand, now blistering within the shape of the rune. "It rejected me."

Kamari took the amulet, her gaze thoughtful and her lips pinched. She smoothed her thumb over the snowflake marker, the last connection to Sefah. Silence stretched between them, as heavy as the words they had exchanged. It squeezed Tetsunah's lungs but there was nothing she could say to make up for the truth; it simply was as it was.

Finally, Kamari dropped the amulet into her lap, firmness taking over her gentle expression. "Why didn't you come looking for him sooner?" she asked. "Why now?"

Tetsunah flinched, ears flattening back, her jewelry clinking with the movement. "I—I can't depend on him for everything. He came out here to be with you, to be unburdened by people's demands. I was just..." *I thought I could do this alone.*

"The lives of your people are at stake!" Kamari shot to her feet, the amulet clutched tightly in her hand. "You didn't think to at least *ask*?"

"My people don't want his help," Tetsunah snapped. Heat flared in her cheeks, anger stirring in her chest. "They come to Aire to get away from him—they're *afraid* of him. They come to me to live somewhere warm, untouched by harsh winters. I can't drag him into that and destroy their trust in me—they were already blaming him when the frostbite disease started spreading. I didn't..." Slowly, the anger began to fade. Tears pricked her eyes, choking her with regret like thorns wound around her throat. "I didn't know what to do. This has never happened before. Why didn't *you* come to me when he disappeared? Or to Xen?"

Kamari stared at her incredulously. "I thought you would know. The amulet is supposed to tell you these things, like it told you Dei was dead."

"So you just assumed I would come to you?"

"It was a mistake!" Kamari hissed, pupils narrowed to slits like those of a cat. "I'm sorry. I should have gone to you, I get it, but I..." Pausing, she sighed and relaxed the tension in her shoulders. She sank back into her seat. "Something isn't right, Tetsunah. I didn't know what to make of it."

Tetsunah said nothing, her throat closed so tightly that she almost couldn't breathe. "I'm sorry," she choked out, tasting the salty tang of her tears as they slid onto her tongue. "I failed you and Sefah. I failed my people. I failed in my duty as the spirit of spring." Kamari was right; there were lives at stake and she was too caught up in her own head to examine all outlets for a solution. She stopped at trying to contact Sefah when she should have sought him out from the very beginning. He was the master of ice. Even if the plague didn't come from him, he would have known what to do about it. No matter how she looked at it, she had failed.

Kamari glanced at the amulet again, her expression unreadable as she studied it. "There's nothing we can do about the past," she murmured. "All we can do now is focus on the present, and I think we're going to need some help if we want to get to the bottom of this." She held out the amulet.

Tetsunah sniffled and wiped away her tears as her gaze attempted to settle on the shimmering gold disk in front of her. Xenah's autumn rune was turned toward her, a collection of elegant swirls and leaf-like patterns that glowed a warm amber and gold. She accepted the amulet. "Okay. I'll reach out to him."

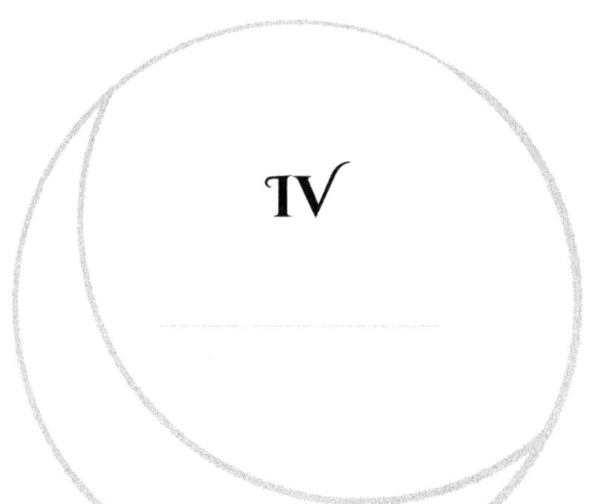

IV

Looking at herself in the mirror was one of the last things Tetsunah wanted to do. Kamari's clothes hung loosely over her thin, short frame. She didn't have the dragonborn woman's broad shoulders, and it was painfully obvious when she was draped in one of her ice-blue tunics. Her own clothes were taken away by Kamari's daughters, Sara and Venni, and her handmaid, Meliv, to be washed while she cleaned herself up. The blue shirt didn't suit her; she yearned for the maroon, light pink, and lavender of her own clothes. The vibrant colors would have drawn attention away from her sad appearance, but now, she was forced to look at it.

Dark, weary circles underlined her normally-bright green eyes, glaringly obvious against her pale skin. The freckles that once dotted the bridge of her nose and cheeks had begun to fade from the lack of sunlight. Without her gold earrings, her broad, pointy ears seemed bare, though that hardly mattered when they only drooped to reflect the heaviness in her heart. Her light brown hair fell freely down her back, loose from its usual braid; the pink tips had gone dull since she spent all her magic traveling, healing, and dividing it in half for Erix.

She had never felt so weak and helpless.

But at least you're clean, something in her retorted. *There's no longer a smell of vomit and blood. That's good, right?*

Though that hardly mattered when people were dying and Sefah was missing—and she couldn't help but feel responsible.

A soft knocking against the door jolted her back to the present. "Tetsunah?" Kamari called from the other side. "Is everything alright? Do the clothes work for you?"

"Yes, everything is fine!" Tetsunah answered, spinning away from the floor length mirror. She took up the indigo sash from the dresser and tied it around her waist, cinching the tunic tight. It still laid awkwardly over her chest, but she resigned herself to her fate and opened the door.

Kamari greeted her with a flicker of a smile, her blue eyes dull with weariness. At her feet was the youngest of her three children, Venni, who clutched Kamari's skirt and stared up at Tetsunah with wide, curious eyes. She had her mother's Draconic features; tiny silver scales dotted her cheeks and a pair of small horns just barely poked out from her black curls. She was the only one of their children that Tetsunah had never met —though she couldn't tell that Koen and Sara remembered her at all.

"Your clothes are set out to dry by the fire," Kamari said. "Meliv told me they should be good as new."

"They *are* good, Mama," Venni affirmed. However, as soon as she had spoken, she stiffened and ducked behind Kamari again.

"Thank you for your help." Tetsunah dipped her head to both of them. "You have been very kind to me."

"It's the least I can do." Kamari quickly waved her thanks away.

"You didn't have to," Tetsunah murmured, remembering the anger blazing in Kamari's eyes. Lowering her head, she rubbed her arm awkwardly. "You could have turned me away."

Venni shuffled out from behind Kamari, having found her

courage again. Her small hand took Tetsunah's, squeezing her fingers tightly. Tetsunah raised her head and met the little girl's gaze. Worry swirled in the depths of her sea-blue eyes. "You're going to bring Papa home, aren't you?" she asked softly.

Kamari's fingers curled at her sides, her lips pressed into a thin line. She said nothing when Tetsunah glanced her way, but she could almost see a similar question reflected in her expression. *You will bring Sefah back, won't you?*

Anxiety gripped Tetsunah, sinking its claws deep into her chest and twisting until her heart ached. She swallowed hard past the lump in her throat. Tears blurred her vision, but she quickly blinked them away. Kneeling down, she took Venni's hands in hers. They were cold, like Sefah's, like those afflicted with the frostbite disease. The thought stirred a flicker of wrongness in her chest, but she quickly stamped it out. "Everything's going to be fine," she said. Her voice came out firm despite the shakiness in her limbs. "We'll bring him back."

A smile curled the corners of Venni's mouth. She nodded, rocking back on her heels. "I know you will."

"Venni." Koen appeared around the corner, hand outstretched to his sister. The rest of his sentence came out in a rush of Draconic words that flew past Tetsunah without meaning. Venni slipped from her grasp and ran to her brother. He took her hand and led her away, casting a quick glance back at them before he and Venni disappeared into another room.

Uncomfortable silence crackled between Tetsunah and Kamari in their absence. Tetsunah pushed to her feet, smoothing the front of her tunic to give her hands something to do. Kamari folded her arms. Her finger tapped a steady rhythm against her long, delicate sleeve.

Tetsunah cleared her throat. "I was hoping to ask you a few more questions about Sefah."

"Yes. Yes, of course." Kamari glanced down the hall the way her children had gone. Venni's laughter drifted through the house, joined by Koen and Sara's teasing. Kamari's face twisted in a frown, silver scales glittering in the lantern light. She gestured to the room Tetsunah had left. "Let's talk in my room."

Together, they shuffled back into the bedroom. Kamari closed the door softly behind them, cutting off the excited squeals of the children as they played. The room was modest. A bed for two took up the far wall, dressed in a thick, dark blue quilt and a white pelt draped over the foot. Two nightstands sat on either side of it; one was empty, while the other housed a lantern and a small vase of flowers—touched by the imprint of Sefah's magic. The dresser and mirror were set out closest to the door. A bookcase lined the bare wall to the right side, though many shelves were empty. Sighing, Kamari leaned against the door.

"Sefah hasn't been gone as long as your people have been suffering," she murmured, running a hand across her face.

Tetsunah pursed her lips. "Did he seem strange to you before he disappeared?"

Kamari hesitated, uncertainty flitting through her pale eyes. She drew her shoulders up and ducked her head, hands folded behind her.

"Kamari?" Tetsunah prompted. "What happened?"

"He was acting strange before he disappeared, yes. He would get up in the middle of the night and pace the house before going to stand outside. I would find him staring at the moon with a blank expression on his face. It was nothing too worrying." She began to twist her ring, head tilted to hide her expression from Tetsunah. "But then, one night he looked me in the eye and asked me what I would do if he was forced to make an evil choice. If he had to commit some atrocious deed."

Tetsunah frowned, her gut twisting. "What did you say?"

"I didn't say anything." Her voice cracked. "I didn't know how to respond so I just waved his question away, but now I can't help but feel that it was connected somehow to why he's gone. He wasn't violent or anything like that. He didn't seem ill either. He just became so… *quiet.* Unfocused. Distant."

Tetsunah pursed her lips. She skimmed her finger across the edge of the dresser. The wood was smooth and sturdy, constructed from dark cedar. A small, glass sculpture sat atop it —a unicorn, its head tossed so that its mane was splayed through the air. Curious, she picked it up. It was cold to the touch. *Ice.* Yet it was unmelted despite the warm air that permeated the house. It was pure, like Sefah's magic, glittering blue with his touch.

"Maybe he was corrupted somehow?" She turned to Kamari, cradling the ice unicorn. "We, the Seasonal Spirits, were born of magic. Perhaps something has darkened his core and he's losing control. Maybe he could feel it and was trying to warn you."

"No," Kamari snapped, eyes flashing. "He would never give himself to dark magic."

"He could be cursed by someone else. Or hurt by some kind of magic weapon, imbued with dark magic like poison."

"*No.* Sefah is no fool. There's no one around here to challenge him either!"

Tetsunah gently set the unicorn back on the dresser. She licked her lips, already dreading the words that formed on the tip of her tongue. It pricked her skin with anxiety, but there was no way to avoid it. Steeling herself, she took a deep breath. "Perhaps he really is angered by the people and this is his way of retaliating. Maybe all of *this* is the evil deed he mentioned."

"Tetsunah." A growl edged Kamari's words, rolling with the aggression the dragonborn were best known for. The woman's gaze was like a pair of twin daggers, digging into Tetsunah's soul. She lifted her chin, her lips quivering though she tried to hide it by pressing them into a firm frown. "Please. Don't say such things about him. He's not a villain."

"I'm sorry," Tetsunah whispered. "I'm only trying to figure out the cause so I can come up with a solution."

Slowly, Kamari relaxed. She twisted her ring again and looked away. "It's not like him. He would never target innocents or create such a destructive storm. Winter is a harsh season by nature, yes, but he doesn't wish to lord over everyone with an iron fist for a cycle. He only ever wants to usher in the natural reset of the world."

"That's why corruption seems most likely to me, or some other kind of loss of control," Tetsunah continued, keeping her voice level and soft. "I don't like the idea, but it would explain why he was acting strange, why he disappeared, and maybe why his magic is running wild."

"The first thing we need to do is find him," Kamari said. "It's the only way we're going to get any answers. When do you think Xenah will be here?"

Tetsunah opened her mouth to speak, but a loud crash interrupted. Giggles floated down the hall, quickly joined by Koen's shouting. Kamari jolted to attention as a pair of heavy boots made their way toward the door.

"Again, again!" Venni called, squealing with laughter.

"I know, I know. Give me a minute. I need to meet with the ladies."

The door swung open to reveal Xenah standing in the hall, his expression stern. His dark skin was flushed, gold eyes narrowed as his brow furrowed. His cinnamon-colored hair was disheveled, shimmering gold tips dulled like the pink in Tetsunah's own. Flurries of snow clung to his hair and clothes, and he was shivering as he stood there.

However, as soon as his gaze shifted to Tetsunah, his expression relaxed and a grin split his lips. "Te-Te!" He crossed into the room, breezing past Kamari without a word. His arms wrapped around Tetsunah and crushed her in a hug before she could argue. "It's good to see you!"

"I've told you before; please don't call me that," she muttered against his shoulder. She tensed awkwardly against him and gave his arm a quick pat.

He pulled away, holding her at arm's length. "Tetsunah's too long. What about Tet?"

Her ears twitched, a frown pulling at her lips. "I can't convince you to use my full name?"

Kamari cleared her throat and stepped forward. "Xenah," she ground out, her smile forced as he turned to her. "Glad you could join us. We have much to talk about."

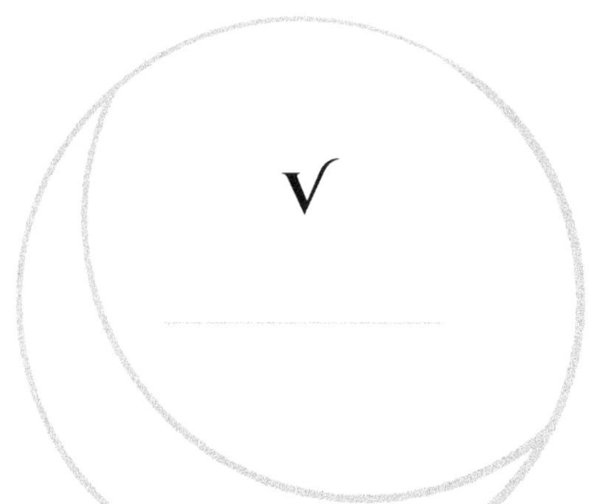

V

They left the bedroom and returned to the sitting room, where the hearth was still burning strong. Heat settled over the room like a soft blanket, soothing the aching cold in Tetsunah's chest—the void left behind by her magic. After a quick word with Kamari, Meliv ushered the children down the hall to their playroom. Venni adamantly refused, digging her heels in and declaring that she wished to play more with Xen, but Koen and Sara were quick to move her along. Meliv trailed after them, glancing knowingly back at Kamari. She had no horns like the silver dragonborn, but the green scales that dotted her cheeks were just as striking. She had also come from Selini's temple as a dragonborn who had abandoned the ways of her people.

As soon as they were gone, Kamari inhaled deeply, rubbing her temples.

"Find a place to sit and make yourself comfortable," she said as she made her way to the hall. "I'll let Tetsunah explain what's going on while I make you some tea."

"No need." Xen dropped himself into the nearest seat, sinking into the plush cushions. He tucked his chin into his maroon scarf, arms folded over his chest. "I already know. It's Sefah. He's the problem."

Kamari stopped in the doorway. Though her face was turned away from them, Tetsunah could feel the distress twisting in the air around her. Tetsunah sank into the chair closest to Xen. "What do you mean?"

Xen glanced at her, golden-amber gaze searching her face. The firelight gave him a warm glow, fitting for the gold aura that encircled him. With a sigh, he leaned forward to rest his elbows on his knees, hands folded. His pointed elf ears twitched and folded down. "I was out in the human kingdom of Sheniir. Many people there have been overcome with a strange sickness, like there's—"

"Ice eating them from the inside out?" Tetsunah echoed. Images resurfaced in her mind; the blue tint to a person's skin, the cracks of frost that split their flesh, the constant shivering despite the fire near them and the blankets wrapped around them. Death came when ice froze their heart completely.

Xenah nodded firmly, a dark look swirling in his eyes.

"The frostbite disease. That's what we call it in Aire." Her thoughts took a sharp turn, zeroing in on Erix and her people tucked away below ground. The emptiness in her core where her magic should have been ached painfully. She rubbed her arms and shifted her eyes to her feet to avoid Xen's stern face. "It has taken many of those I hold dear."

"I'm sorry, Tet," he murmured. Pity softened the tone of his voice, dropping it to a pitch so low she almost missed it. His hand brushed her arm in an awkward show of comfort. The touch lingered for a moment before he pulled away. "Sefah was there—in Sheniir. He was casually surveying the frozen bodies of those already dead. When I called out to him, he barely looked at me before he vanished." Xen clenched his fists, jaw tight. "Why would he run if he has nothing to hide?"

"What are you suggesting?" Kamari turned to face him, the

strings of blue jewels tied between her horns swinging, and planted her fist against her hip.

"I'm *suggesting* that Sefah is abusing his power as the winter spirit to kill hundreds—maybe thousands—of people and disrupt the balance we're supposed to maintain between the seasons. The amulet showed me the same thing. It's time we take action." Xen pushed to his feet and summoned his sword in a shower of amber sparks. "We have to kill him."

"Absolutely not!" Tetsunah shot out of her seat, hands warming as a faint trickle of her magic oozed to the surface. Dizziness washed over her, and she steadied herself against the curved arm of the chair. Gritting her teeth, she pinned her glare on Xen, hoping he couldn't see the exhaustion in her face. "There has to be another way, another explanation. It's not like him!"

"That's precisely why we can't let him continue, and why I don't believe he's going to listen to a friendly chat over tea." Xen tied the sword sheath to his waist. It was a pointed effort to keep his face averted from her, she noticed. "He's not himself, and he doesn't seem to have any intent to come to himself soon. This won't end unless we take matters into our own hands. We have to kill him."

"And you got all of this from one encounter?" Kamari scoffed. "Don't be rash, autumn spirit. Perhaps it's *you* who isn't thinking clearly."

Xen's eyes flashed as he looked her way. "You don't know what I saw. This is the only way."

"Do you even hear yourself?" Tetsunah snapped. Anger pricked her skin, fanning a flame deep inside her. "He's not a wild animal, Xen. He's our *friend*. I won't let that happen; there *has* to be another way."

"He wouldn't turn on us," Kamari added. Xen drew his sword, but she quickly slammed her hand against his, shoving the blade back into the sheath. "Xenah, listen to me. You know him. You know this isn't right."

Xen paused for a moment, glancing between Tetsunah and Kamari. Something flickered in the depths of his gaze. Straightening his back, he brushed Kamari aside. "I'll do whatever it takes to protect my family," he said. "I can't lose you, not like I lost Dei."

Family. The word struck a cord deep within Tetsunah. Deiah and Xenah were her family, the friends she had always had. Kamari was her family as well, along with Koen, Sara, and Venni. The people of Aire were her family. If she wished to protect them, she needed to find Sefah.

But he was her family, too. He was the one that smiled most warmly at her, even though his hands were always cold and his eyes were a piercing shade of ultramarine. Frost dusted his fingers, strikingly white against his bronze skin. He spoke softly, always careful, always gentle. Though winter was vicious and cruel, he was not. He never had been; she couldn't imagine he ever would be.

In her mind, she saw Xen's blade through his heart. Crimson blood stained the pure white snow he loved so much, tainting the air with the stench of death. Kamari wept for his loss, shattered by grief and pain. Xen looked in horror at what he had done, and he no longer held that insistent, righteous glint in his gaze. The vision blurred as tears filled Tetsunah's eyes, but when she blinked, it was gone. She was in the present still, faced with Xen's unwavering stare and Kamari's pleading expression.

She lifted her chin, nails digging into her palms as she curled her fists tight. "That's not protecting your family," she said firmly. "That's destroying it."

"Moreover," Kamari said, jabbing her finger at Xen's chest. "You will *not* come into my house and suggest murdering my husband in front of my children."

Xen brushed her hand away and gestured down the hall. "They're not even here!"

"Do you think that stops them from trying to find somewhere to lurk and listen?"

"I'm just saying that you have to be open to the possibility," Xen argued. Desperation edged his voice, twinging it with a painful note of melancholy. "I *saw* him. He's not himself. When was the last time you spoke with him?"

Kamari hesitated. Her lips parted, but no response came. Clamping them shut again, she turned her face away, black curls and silver tinsel obscuring her expression.

This isn't right. A flicker of wrongness stirred in Tetsunah's chest, something dark and disturbing. It left a foul taste in her mouth, and she swallowed hard against it. She recalled the amulet and the disrupted aura in Sefah's rune, the unnatural cold leaking out from it. Frowning, she pressed her fist to her lips, her brows knitting together. The storm was violent. The sickness was violent. The magic was violent and out of control. *But killing him?* "I want to see him before I make a decision about what to do. Do you have any idea where he might be?"

Xen shook his head. "You know as well as I do that he's a master of the warp spell. After leaving Sheniir, he could have gone anywhere."

"When were you in Sheniir?"

"Just before you reached out to me. I was there with Rym doing some surveillance. That *lovely* ice storm of Sefah's chased Rym out of his home."

Rym was a sun dragon raised by Deiah while she was alive. Since her passing, Xen had taken up caring for him. He was as reclusive as Dei had been, but was no doubt just as unnerved by the sudden onslaught of cold as they were. Like the sun, he couldn't shine as brightly under the full force of winter's wrath. "Is Rym still here?"

"Went to the Senn Deserts in Draconic territory to see if it's as bad out there as it is here. He plans to circle back here after."

Cold fear slithered down Tetsunah's spine. With a shiver, she wrapped her arms around herself. Never before had she wished so desperately for the touch of magic, to be wrapped in its warmth and hidden away in its protection. Only a faint pull responded to her summons, dusting her fingertips in pale pink sparks. It could do little more than glitter in the light and vanished just as quickly.

Kamari's hand brushed her shoulder, jolting her out of her thoughts. The woman's lips were pursed, her face creased with worry. "What are you thinking, Tetsunah?"

"If Xen was hostile when they met, then turned and went straight to Sefah's home..." she murmured. "Do you think he would follow him here?"

Silence followed, as loaded as her question had been. Kamari and Xen shared a glance, but neither spoke.

A sudden chill permeated the air, sharper than any blade. It pricked Tetsunah's skin, digging claws deep into her flesh until she could swear it would draw forth blood. Shivering, she exhaled a shaky breath, watching it fog in front of her face. "Xen—"

A gust of icy wind rattled the walls, snuffing out the fire in the hearth and throwing Tetsunah's vision into the dark. Somewhere in the house, Venni screamed. Wood floorboards creaked as Kamari fled the room. Soothing draconic words floated down the hall.

Xenah cursed and spun away, metal scraping metal as he drew his sword. He flung the door open, flooding the dark room with silver moonlight and opening it up to the full blast of the icy wind. Snow forced its way inside and covered the floor in a stark white coat. Xenah stepped out without another word, slamming the door so hard it shook the wall.

Tetsunah's heart stuttered, her feet frozen as a whirl of panic and fear seized her mind. The world spun, the air suddenly too thin to fill her lungs. As her gaze shifted, she spotted her cloak hanging over the empty fireplace. She snatched it up and swung it over her shoulders. It was still damp, warm from the fire yet heavy with water, but she didn't care. She gripped its edges, pulling them tight over her chest, and raced outside after Xen.

Wind and snow assaulted her. Her bare feet sank into the powder, bitter cold nipping at her exposed skin until she grew numb to the sensation. The day had passed while she was inside, and night reigned again. Shadows draped the world in a veil of blackness, broken only by the moonlight glistening against the pure white snow. Shielding her face, she stumbled through the snow until she made it to Xenah.

He stood frozen, body tensed while his neck was craned to peer at something in the sky. His hand gripped his sword so tightly that his knuckles paled. The wind tugged at his hair and coat, the embroidered tail of his scarf billowing out behind him. Tetsunah followed his gaze to the inky black sky.

Floating gracefully in the air, a perfect silhouette against the light of the crescent moon, was Sefah. One half of his face was concealed beneath his indigo wrap, the edge embroidered in a pattern that resembled frost. His white hair stuck out from beneath it, a striking sight against his dark skin. He looked down on them with only one eye visible—the eye that glowed with the snowflake rune, sight restored as the temperature dropped to the frigid depths. He carried no weapons, but the air around him pulsed dangerously with magic. He narrowed his eye, the white glow brightening, and tilted his chin, lips pinched in a tight frown.

Sefah. A dizzying mix of relief and fear twisted together in Tetsunah's gut. His aura was frenzied, disturbingly chaotic like his rune inside the amulet. Xen was right. Something was wrong.

"Lord of winter," she addressed him, her words slurred by

the cold and choppy through her chattering teeth. "I'm glad to see you. I—I was worried about you. We need your help." She stepped toward him.

Xen's arm blocked her path. When she looked at him, he shook his head.

Sefah descended from his perch in the air, his black boots alighting gracefully upon the snow. "Tetsunah, Xenah." He raised his hand, fingers splayed toward her. Flecks of magic danced at the tips of his fingers, which were permanently marked by a web of white cracks. Usually, his hands were perfectly steady. Now, there was a slight tremor as they hung in the air. His voice quivered as he spoke. "Do not interfere," he said.

The air crackled as an ice spike took shape in front of him. Uncertainty flickered across his expression. When he moved, the motions were stiff and awkward. Taking the spike in his hand, he pulled back his arm and thrust it like a spear. It hurtled toward Tetsunah in a straight arc.

"Get down!" Xen threw himself against her, wrapping his arms around her to shield her. Snow cushioned their fall, but its merciless chill sank deeper into Tetsunah's bones. As soon as the spike whizzed over their heads and shattered against the ground, Xen shot to his feet. A growl built in the back of his throat. Raising his sword, he raced at Sefah with a shout.

"Xen, don't!" Tetsunah scrambled to her feet, but her legs gave way beneath her. "Please, you know this isn't right!"

If he heard her cries above the howling wind, he didn't stop. He swung his sword in a wide arc, aimed for Sefah's neck. The winter spirit lifted his arm, ice coating it in a thick shield. The blade crashed against the ice. A loud *clash* rang through the air between them. Calmly, Sefah took hold of the blue threads of his magic, twisting them around his fingers. A second spike of ice formed at his command; Xen leapt back from it, keeping his body tensed to dodge.

"Please, stay away. I don't want to hurt you," Sefah whispered, voice pleading. However, when he faced Xenah, his one visible eye scrutinized him. He lifted the spike, and Xen shifted. Sefah's gaze darted to Tetsunah, his face contorted as if the motion pained him. The snowflake rune in his eye brightened as it settled on her. "Stay away." For the second time, he hurled the razor sharp weapon at her.

Time seemed to slow. Xen turned in horror, realization dawning in his amber eyes. Tetsunah watched, frozen in fear. Every inch of her mind screamed at her body to move, but she couldn't find the strength. The cold smothered her, choking her. She couldn't breathe; she couldn't think. She couldn't move. *Stay away.* His warning echoed through her mind, loud above the chaotic buzz that clouded her.

"Tetsunah!"

Xen leapt between her and the spike, his sword forgotten in the snow. The icicle sliced his side as it zipped through; blood splattered the ground, bright red against white. Diverted from its course, the spike of ice crashed into the snow mere inches from Tetsunah's face. It shattered into a shower of blue sparks. Xen crashed to the ground, blood pouring from the gash in his side. A scream ripped through the air—Tetsunah didn't realize it was hers until her throat began to burn.

She shot to his side, ripping her cloak from her shoulders and pressing it against the wound. He hissed, his body rigid against the pressure.

Ahead, Sefah dropped his hand back to his side. The wind ripped his wrap away from his face, exposing wide, tear-filled eyes—one glowing white with the rune, the other barely visible in the dark. His shoulders trembled as he pushed them back, lifting his chin. "I'm sorry. Please, Tet, stay away from me," he croaked. "You cannot interfere."

In the next instant, he vanished, leaving the heavy warning hanging in the air between them.

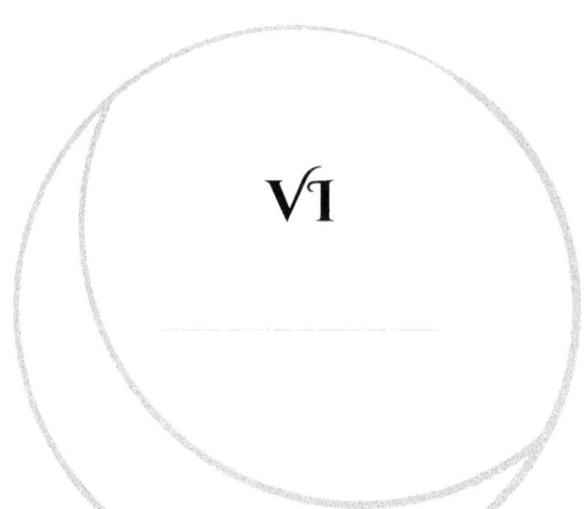

VI

" I 'm sorry," was the only thing Tetsunah could find the strength to say. Tears streaked her cheeks, and her throat closed so tightly that she almost couldn't get the words out at all. She squeezed Xenah's hand, pressing his knuckles to her forehead. "I'm sorry, Xen."

"It's alright. It's not your fault," he reassured her again, always ready with the same response. If she looked at him, she knew she would find that soothing smile on his face, but she refused to lift her head.

She stood beside him in the sitting room, head bowed to keep her watery gaze locked on her feet. Though it had been an hour or so since she brought Xen inside, she could still feel the bite of cold deep inside her. It clung to her bones, turning her fingers red. A heavy blanket draped from her shoulders, her cloak having been taken away by Meliv to be scrubbed clean again. It reeked of blood, stained beyond recognition. Meliv seemed confident she could get it back to normal and left after tossing a comforting smile Tetsunah's way. Koen lit the fire in the hearth before Kamari dismissed him. It was warm, but not enough to keep the image of Sefah's empty gaze from boring into her, pumping icy fear into her blood.

Kamari tied off the bandages wrapped around Xen's side. "That should be good. Try not to move around too much," she said as she collected the bloody cloths used to clean the wound and disposed of them. When she turned back to the tea table, she rolled up the remaining bandages and shut them away in a wooden box. As the lid closed, it cut off the bitter scent of dried herbs. Kamari lifted the box. "I'll leave the two of you alone."

As soon as the sound of her footsteps faded, the air began to crackle with awkward tension. Xen's hand slipped from Tetsunah's. He cleared his throat. Anxiety thrummed in Tetsunah's mind, oozing from every thought that rose to the surface. *It's my fault,* her mind whispered over and over. *I couldn't move. He's hurt because of me.* Cautiously, she peered at Xen through her pink-tipped bangs.

He sat in the plush chair closest to the tea table, leaning back into it and sprawling his legs out in front of him—one foot crossed lazily over the other. The white bandages were painfully obvious against his tan skin, but that was better than the sight of a bloody wound cut into his torso. If the pain bothered him, he didn't show it. Instead, his eyes were distant, his nose scrunched in thought and his lips pursed. Even when Tetsunah brought him inside and Kamari cleaned and bandaged the wound, he didn't flinch or fuss about the pain. He only spoke when Tetsunah fumbled another apology; his response was just as scripted as her statement was.

Sefah's betrayal had dampened Kamari's mood as well. Her pale eyes had glistened with the sheen of tears while she'd worked, her hands trembling the whole time. It was no wonder she'd left in such a rush the moment she was done. There was no way to make it clearer than it already was.

Sefah had turned on them. Sefah had unleashed the wrath of winter. Sefah was the reason everything had gone wrong. *Do not interfere,* he said, as cold as the storm that raged around them. Yet his voice quivered with fear as he added, *I'm sorry, Tet.*

Tetsunah chewed at her lip. She couldn't determine whether he was working of his own accord or not. When he looked at her, his face was almost too empty, too distant. It didn't match the tone of his voice, nor the way his hands trembled when he lifted them. He had always had a knack for being difficult to read when he wanted to be, but he never looked so blank. There was always a hint of the truth in his eyes, hidden behind the white snowflake rune and buried in the depths of ultramarine, but it was always there. This time, however, there was nothing. Even when tears welled in his eyes, she couldn't see the truth through them.

Perhaps it wasn't so clear after all.

Exhaustion formed a pounding headache behind her eyes. *I need to think about something else.* Rising to her feet, she smoothed the front of her tunic. The ice blue color was painfully similar to the one Sefah was wearing; she forced herself to jerk her gaze away.

"Do you… want to lie down?" she asked as she looked at Xen. "I—I might have enough magic to help shrink the wound so that it will heal faster. I can't heal it fully. I spent all my magic to get here, and it won't regenerate in this cold." The words tumbled from her lips in a blur, pouring out one after another like the constant stream of tears that made her vision waver. She sucked in a sharp breath and swiped at her tears. "I'm sorry. I wish I could do more. I'm so sorry."

"It's alright, Tetsunah." Xen rested his elbows against his knees, folding his hands together. "I'm okay, really. It's not that serious. The ice just nicked me." His darkened gaze fell on the windows opposite them that faced the winter storm raging outside. Flecks of snow clung to the glass, tiny spots of white against the pitch black sky.

"Please. I want to help you."

"You don't have to."

"It's my fault you got hurt, so I—"

"*It's not your fault.*" Xen snapped his gaze to her, golden eyes blazing. He sighed, and his gaze softened back to its usual warm amber. Shifting in his seat, he edged closer and took her hands. "It's not your fault, Tet. Stop blaming yourself. *Sefah* made this choice; he's the one to blame."

"I should have stayed inside." Tetsunah sank back to her knees at the foot of his chair, pressing his hands to her forehead. Her loose, unbraided hair spilled over her shoulders in a mess of light brown tangles. "If I wasn't there, he wouldn't have attacked me and you wouldn't have gotten in the way."

"I would do anything to protect you," he murmured. "I don't regret that you were there or what I did. Sefah is…" Another sigh escaped him. "It's unlike him to target you, but I know how he fights. This is the kind of thing he does when he knows the enemy."

The tears began anew as a sob built up in her throat. "I don't want to blame him. I don't *want* to be against him."

"Tetsunah, look at me."

She raised her head. Now, exhaustion and sadness darkened Xen's face. The hand that held hers suddenly seemed fragile, just as shaky and uncertain as her own.

"I'm sorry that it has to be this way," he said. "No matter what happens, I'm with you."

"Well, I won't let it end this way." Kamari had returned to the doorway, her arms folded over a sleek, silver breastplate. A sword hung from the sash around her waist, its ornate sheath painted with Draconic runes. She pulled her black curls back, careful not to catch her horns as she tied her hair into a ponytail. Shoving away from the wall, her steps confident and purposeful, she made her way to them. "I'm going after him. Xenah, you should stay. Meliv will continue to tend to your wound; the two of you can watch the children. I'll come back with Sefah or not at all."

Tetsunah shot to her feet, eyes wide as she faced Kamari. "You can't go by yourself. Something isn't right with him, Kamari. He'll fight you if you follow!"

"If it's a fight he wants, it's a fight he'll get," Kamari sneered, her lip curling back to reveal fangs. Tetsunah shrank back on instinct. Though she had abandoned the violent ways of her people long ago, Kamari was still a dragonborn at her core. Her silver scales and horns were a daily reminder, but they became easy to overlook when she was calm, like the soft roll of the ocean's waves. Now, she was a storm, waves that thrashed against the shore and threatened to pull anyone into the deep end.

"I won't play games with him. I was once one of Goddess Selini's top disciples, her Head Dragonborn. I can handle a little ice. Also..." She slammed her hands against the table—even Xen jumped that time. Leaning close, she lowered her voice to a hiss. "I'm his wife," she snapped. "If there's anyone who should be able to get him back to his senses, it's me."

Tetsunah chewed her lip, twisting the hem of her tunic. Anger simmered in the very air around Kamari, but even it could not hide the pain in her eyes. Tetsunah pulled at the fabric wrapped around her fingers. "I understand that you're upset, but—"

Xen chuckled, a lopsided grin working its way to his lips. He leaned back in his chair and threw his arms back behind his head. "I like this Kamari better. I'm going with you."

Surprise flickered across Kamari's face, but Tetsunah found she couldn't share it. Instead, the fight within her sputtered out, shrinking to a tiny bud in the very back of her mind. Exhaustion quickly filled the empty space it had left, and Tetsunah pinched the bridge of her nose, squeezing her eyes shut. A retort formed on the tip of her tongue, but she swallowed it. It was no use. Once his mind was set on something, Xen was nearly impossible to deter. She had no right to deny Kamari either. She deserved to be angry; she deserved to chase Sefah and demand answers. *But...*

"I'm coming," Tetsunah said. "I'm worried about Sefah, and I promised my people that I would find a way to save them. Moreover..." She frowned and pinned her glare on Xen. "Someone has to keep you from overexerting your wound."

He shrugged innocently and splayed his fingers. "Hey, I have magic too, you know. I'm not a healer, but I can keep the energy focused on the wound so it doesn't hinder me. I just won't be able to use my power for anything else."

"Not that you use it much anyway." Kamari wrinkled her nose. "You've always been the least skilled with magic out of the four."

"I have a lot of power. I simply choose only to use it for my duty as the spirit of autumn."

Tetsunah cleared her throat in an effort to drag the conversation back on track. "I suggest we wait until morning. It's too dark to travel right now, and it may be a bit warmer once the sun is out. Do you have an idea where Sefah might have gone?" she asked as she faced Kamari again.

She nodded firmly, her face grave. Tilting her head, she jerked her chin at the window across from them. "The eye of the storm," she said. "If he wants to be alone, he'll go to the Aurora Range."

Tetsunah stiffened, swallowing past the lump in her throat. The frigid wasteland that made up the northernmost mountains was the heart of Sefah's territory, the place where he was created. His power would be strongest there, the cold more vicious than any other place the storm had touched.

Sucking in a sharp breath, she steeled herself. "Then that's where we'll go."

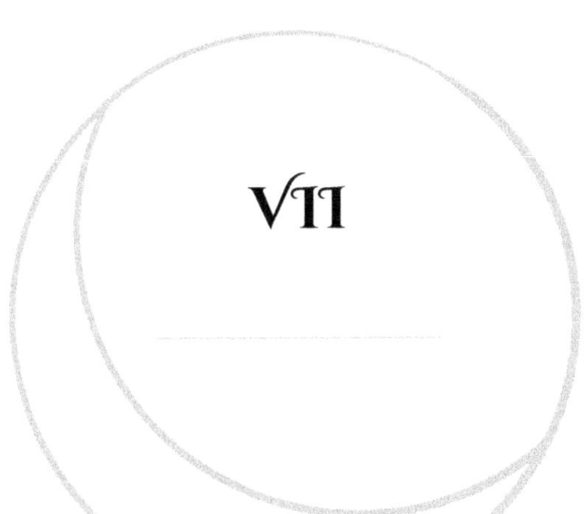

VII

Tetsunah proposed that they leave just after sunrise, allowing everyone a few hours to rest and gather their thoughts. Though reluctant, Kamari and Xen both finally agreed. Xen even offered to call Rym back so they wouldn't have to walk all the way to the Aurora Range. Once their plans were set, Kamari and Meliv prepared the guest room. Xen promptly fell asleep on the seating room sofa, leaving the guest room to Tetsunah, who had no choice but to accept it.

"I'll make sure your clothes are ready for you by morning," Meliv said as she spread a second blanket over the bed. Her brown hair was still tossed up in a loose bun, her dark eyes glittering in the candlelight. When she turned to Tetsunah, a flicker of a smile found its way to her face. "If you need anything, I'll be down the hall. Please don't hesitate to ask for help."

"Thank you, Meliv." Tetsunah returned the smile, but it faltered and quickly dropped. She turned away before Meliv left the room, unable to face her properly when her mind was still reeling from the encounter with Sefah. The door closed softly after a moment, letting her know that Meliv had moved on.

The room was peaceful. Silence reigned and removed Tetsunah from the nightly activities of the rest of the house. In some ways, it reminded her of the stillness of her home back in Aire, which would have brought comfort under normal circumstances. Now, it left her skin crawling as her mind began to drift back to Sefah's trembling, frightened figure. The moon had haloed him in its pale light; it'd made him appear small yet unearthly. He wasn't the Sefah she knew, the Sefah she depended on. *So what happened to that Sefah?*

Her vision began to blur with tears as thorny vines sealed her throat shut, winding tighter and tighter like a snake—but there was nothing there when she put her hands to her neck. Sniffling, she wiped her eyes and took a deep breath. *Calm, Tetsunah. Ground yourself. Think about something else.*

The floor beneath her was carpeted, soft against the soles of her feet. It was a black fur rug that spread up to the edge of the bed. Under it was the same wood floor as the rest of the house. She padded forward and brushed her hand against the bedpost. Smooth wood, sanded to perfection. She turned her gaze to the rest of the room. It was quaint with a single bed and a wardrobe, but no other furniture. With the knowledge that Sefah and Kamari hosted very few guests, this came as no surprise. They had no real reason to put such care into a room no one would ever rest in. And yet, a shelf above the bed toted several more of Sefah's ice trinkets, which offered the dark room some inch of character and comfort. Even here, she was depending on him to bring everything together.

Sighing, she sank against the edge of the bed, its cream-colored blankets folding beneath her. A candle sat atop the nightstand, its flame burning strong though it had shrunk the wax down to the size of her thumb. The light flickered and cast long shadows across the walls that danced in time with the flame. Dei used to say that the dance of fire was the purest form of freedom and magic. Xen always rolled his eyes at her, and

Sefah would argue that it couldn't be free as long as it was connected to a source.

"If it's magic, it isn't free," he would say in his calm, sage-like voice. *"Magic is bound to the will of its user. A user bound to the will of magic has no right to its power."*

"I think you're just saying whatever comes to mind to contradict me," Dei argued, a sly smile curling her lips. *"It's unflattering. Admit defeat graciously for once."*

"He doesn't know the meaning," Xen laughed.

The memory trickled away with the echo of better days left in its wake. Tetsunah had nothing to say then, and nothing she said now would reach any of them. It would be better to stop dwelling on things out of reach, but the flame's light kept its grip on her. Magic or not, its brilliance was the ghost of Dei's.

All at once, exhaustion slammed into her like waves crashing against the shore. She slumped back against the bed and stared blankly at the ceiling overhead as her mind slowly began to numb. *Sefah,* some part of her reached out. She could just barely see the faint blue thread of his magic; she twined it around her fingers. *What's happening, old friend?*

The air cooled, a chill slithering down her arm, but there was no response. She held on until her eyes drooped shut and she couldn't hold on anymore.

* * *

TETSUNAH WASN'T sure how long she slept before a faint whisper brushed the back of her mind. It wrapped around the tendrils of her consciousness and pulled until she fell back to the waking world. The tender caress lingered with an icy prick. *"Tetsunah,"* it called, echoing as if it came from a great distance. *"Tet, are you there?"*

Startled, she jerked upright, a gasp wrenched from her lips. The candle had gone out, draping the room in the cover of darkness. Only a flickering blue light was visible on her night-stand. It beat in a constant rhythm, like a heart, as it filled the room with the thick touch of magic.

"Tet?" The icy magic pulled at her. *"Please answer me. I swear I mean you no harm."*

Recognition spilled over her reservations. In a flash, she scrambled over the bed to get to the nightstand, where her amulet lay beside the burnt out stump of wax. Meliv had left it there, she remembered, after taking it out of her cloak's pocket. It glowed blue like Sefah's rune, pulsing in a steady beat. The snowflake-shaped scar on her palm throbbed in the same rhythm. Without thinking, she snatched up the small gold disk and sank back into the bed. It didn't take long to slip into the bond this time, opening up the golden stage much faster than before. This time, Xen was asleep, huddled over the autumn rune and snoring soundly. She turned and found Sefah standing in his corner of the stage, gaze fixed on her. He was a ghostly blue figure, constructed of the essence of his magic, but he was there. For the first time in months, he was there.

Her initial relief faded, overturned by apprehension. Fear pricked her skin, and she shrank back from him, throwing a quick glance at the polished gold beneath them. Cracks still marred the surface of the giant amulet, split apart by vicious spikes of ice like the one that pierced Xen's side. Flecks of snow hung in the air, and frost crept closer to her and Xen's side of the stage.

"Where have you been?" she snapped, fingers curling at her sides as she lifted her gaze to meet Sefah's. Thorny vines sprang to life from the trickle of magic that remained in her core and slowly wound up her arms. "No, better yet, what's going on?"

"I'm sorry." He echoed their previous encounter, pointed ears drooping. His head was uncovered this time, exposing his snow-white hair and cool bronze skin. He fidgeted with the hem of his wrap, which settled around his shoulders like a scarf. "I truly am. I wish I could have done more."

"Answer the question, Sefah." She softened her gaze slightly, relaxing the knot in her brow. "Please."

"Something's wrong, Tet." He turned and began to pace. The movement shed glittering sparks of magic from his form. They drifted aimlessly and vanished before touching the frost-covered ground. "It's like I've completely lost control of winter. Some days, I can't even control myself. It's controlling *me*, Tet. Possessing me."

"Possessing you?" she murmured. Confusion welled up inside her, dark and bubbling with anxiety. "It can do that?"

Still pacing, Sefah turned sharply and stalked across the snowflake rune that stretched across his corner of the amulet. His steps were silent, but she could almost hear the slap of his boots against the gold ringing in her ears. She flattened them, pursing her lips, and tried to bury the sliver of unease that ate away at her insides.

"I need you and Xenah to stay away from me," he said finally, lifting his gaze to meet hers. It burned with certainty this time, free of the shaky fear that consumed him before. Startling clarity took hold of his brilliant blue eyes, like the ocean sparkling in the silver moonlight. The look hardened into something icy, and he jerked his face away, breathing a deep sigh. "I don't want to hurt you more than I already have. I can't risk that in my current state." Jaw tight, he glared down his frost-coated fingers. "I swear I'll get this under control. Promise you will keep my family safe until then. And… tell Kamari I'm sorry."

Anger burned in Tetsunah's chest. The vines tightened around her arms as they sprouted fiery red blossoms. "Do you not realize the damage you've already caused? *Multitudes* are dead, Sefah. Winter is destroying Calistie—perhaps all of Anticuus. I can't turn a blind eye and just ignore what's happening while you try to fix it yourself. I *won't!*"

Magic flared to life around her, swirling in a rose-dusted storm that brewed with the anger inside her. It ripped the petals from her vines and pulled at her loose hair. Wild strands of brown-and-pink locks billowed around her. Something pulled sharply at her core, and she gritted her teeth. *Calm. You don't have that kind of power to waste on your emotions.*

Sefah winced as if she had struck him, the softness in his expression giving way to something hurt—regretful, almost. He pressed his lips into a thin line as his frost-coated fingers curled at his sides. "I know," he murmured. "I swear to you, Tetsunah, I can fix this. I can regain control, but you have to trust me to be able to do this alone."

Calm. Tetsunah took a deep breath, waiting until the throbbing behind her eyes dulled. She glanced at him. Unlike before, he didn't seem violent or unstable. He appeared more like himself, albeit small and fragile. Her hands itched to take hold of his, to squeeze his fingers and offer him what little comfort she could. He didn't deserve to suffer; he didn't deserve to isolate himself, and yet he always tried to. Swallowing hard, she slowly crept toward him.

All at once, ice shot up from the ground and blocked her path. Sefah leapt back like a frightened cat, his eyes wide as they flitted about. Cold nipped at Tetsunah's face, and she clenched her teeth against its vicious bite. It shoved against her, and her feet slipped, throwing her back to her corner of the stage.

Stumbling, she righted herself, spinning to face him again. Indignation flared to life in her chest, and she shot forward, only to be slammed back by the ice again. Her back hit the floor, and the air in her lungs left in a whoosh. Gasping, she pushed herself upright. "You don't have to do this on your own!" she cried. Beyond the growing wall of ice, his ghostly form flickered. "Let us help you, Sefah. It's our duty as spirits, but it's not just that. We're your friends. We care about you."

"No," he snapped, the white rune in his eye flashing dangerously. Pain splintered his twisted expression, and he doubled over, drawing a hiss from his lips as he pressed a hand to the eye. For a moment, he stayed that way as the sound of his labored breathing occupied the empty silence between them. With a rasp, he said, "Stay away, Tetsunah. Please. I don't want to hurt you."

"Really? Then why did you threaten me back there?" Narrowing her eyes, she threw her arms out in a sweeping gesture toward Xen on the other side of the amulet. "It seemed pretty clear to me then."

"I knew Xen would get in the way. You were never going to be the one that got hurt, and I'm sorry that he had to take the fall." He unraveled the scarf around his neck and draped it over his head to cover half his face. The white rune in his eye brightened, consuming the darkness of the amulet in a blinding whiteness. Again, his voice had shifted to something cold and distant. "It was the only way to stop him from attacking me."

Puzzled, Tetsunah twisted the hem of her shirt, wracking her mind for an explanation, but nothing emerged. Sefah turned, and she opened her mouth to stop him. The cry died in her throat as a hand clamped down on her shoulder.

"Tetsunah!" a distant voice cried, broken by tears. Nails dug into Tetsunah's shoulders, shaking her. "Wake up."

With the wave of his hand, Sefah cut off their connection and wrenched the amulet out from under her. Tetsunah jolted back to reality with a gasp, startled to find Kamari's panic-stricken face so close to her own. Her black hair hung in loose, tangled curls, messy as they framed her face. Her silver breastplate was gone; instead, she was dressed in her nightclothes, which made her appear small. Tears welled in the dragonborn's crystal blue eyes, and she pulled back quickly, swiping at her eyes.

"It's Venni," she explained. Though she tried to hide it, her voice still quivered and her hands were shaking. "She's… freezing. You have to come see her."

"Freezing?" Dazed, still partly clinging to the amulet's hold, the word slipped by without meaning. Tetsunah fumbled with it, desperate to mold it into something. It clicked all too suddenly, and her mind flooded with images of the victims of the frostbite plague. Blue fingers. Ice covered skin. Constant tremors. Cold to the touch. She shoved off the bed and met Kamari's panicked look with a firm stare. "Take me to her."

Kamari nodded, lips quivering as she sniffed. She swept aside, her robe swishing around her feet as she turned. "This way." She paused in the doorway for a quick glance back, but her gaze never made it to Tetsunah. It lingered on the window which faced the distant snowy mountains. Lifting her chin, she left the room in a hurry.

Tetsunah followed, stumbling after her. Though the house was warm, her skin crawled—perhaps a lingering touch of the cold that opposed her within the amulet. *Or maybe it's just your fear.*

They emerged from the guest room into the main hallway that branched off into each of the bedrooms, save for Kamari and Sefah's room. Eerie silence permeated the air. Xen's snoring had stopped, and for once, Tetsunah missed it. Wooden floorboards creaked beneath her bare feet, and she winced, startled by the noise. Her skin crawled with unease, and it seemed to take an eternity to cross the hallway.

The house was dark, save for the girls' room: a beacon, as evident by the flickering light that slid out from underneath the door. Kamari gently pushed it open, and the light flooded the hall. Meliv perched on the edge of Venni's bed against the left wall while Sara huddled sniffling in her own bed on the opposite side. Venni lay against her pillows, brow wrinkled and eyes shut as she heaved in shuddering breaths. Blue veins of ice spiderwebbed beneath her olive skin, a perfect mirror of the symptoms Tetsunah had seen countless times before. Her heart wrenched in her chest, and she stalled in the doorway. Venni lifted her hand, groaning. Speaking in soothing whispers, Meliv took her hand and stroked the back of it with her thumb.

"She was fine earlier today," Kamari said, pacing the room as she chewed her nails. "I put the girls to bed, and a few hours later, Sara comes to me saying Venni can't breathe."

"S—she kept saying she was freezing." Sara tucked herself behind the cover of her blankets until all Tetsunah could see was the top of her head, her black hair knotted from sleep. "When I touched her, she was like ice."

Tetsunah clenched her jaw as a flicker of panic shot through her. Still, she lifted her chin and strode into the room, forcing confidence into her steps. They didn't need someone lost and afraid. Those who were hurting needed someone strong to lean on. She was the spirit of spring, the leader of Aire. She would be strong.

"Step away from her, please." Gently, she lifted Venni's hand from Meliv's grasp, resting her own against the woman's back. When Meliv's startled glance landed on her, she smiled reassuringly. "Allow me to take a look."

Meliv hesitated a moment longer before looking to Kamari, who nodded. Sighing, Meliv stood and left the side of the bed.

Tetsunah settled beside Venni. She didn't even stir as Tet sank into the bed, the girl's eyes squeezed tightly shut. Her skin was ice cold against Tetsunah's, but the blue cracks had not yet risen to the surface and split her skin. She was still in the early stages, but Tetsunah had no way to know how long she would last. She had never dealt with a dragonborn patient before—but even elf and human children didn't last long under the curse of the frostbite plague.

Regret tied down her tongue, binding it behind her teeth. A heavy weight crashed down on her shoulders, the same one that always emerged when faced with a mother and her dying child. The truth was there, plain as day, and she owed it to Kamari to confirm it. Yet she couldn't. Confirming it was dooming Venni to an agonizing death at the hands of an incurable disease, a curse that spawned from the wrath of winter.

The very same winter Sefah was supposed to control.

Promise you will keep my family safe until then. How was she supposed to keep them safe from the frigid beast she had no way to calm?

"Tetsunah?" Kamari's voice was soft, a dam that barely held back the waters of her rage. It was always there, teetering on the edge. She was once a Head Dragonborn for a reason.

Tetsunah hung her head as her throat tightened. "It's the frostbite plague. I'm so sorry, Kamari. I—" Her breath hitched and tears pricked her eyes. "I brought it here. I should never have come."

"No."

Tetsunah's head snapped up. In the months she had served as healer against the frostbite plague, she had never seen someone so conflicted. Rage flickered through Kamari's pale eyes, dampened by sadness and weariness, yet she stood perfectly still. Calm radiated off her, but it was not enough to hide the pain that twisted her features. Her silver scales flashed in the light as she moved, bending down to kiss Venni's forehead.

"I know who to blame," Kamari murmured. A feeble smile split her lips as she stroked Venni's cheek. "It can't wait until morning. We have to go after Sefah."

Tetsunah shot to her feet. "No. Xen and I will go. You should stay with your children."

Kamari's gaze slid her way, her pupils narrowed like slits. She righted herself slowly. "Sara," she said. "Please go with Meliv and find Koen."

Sara stiffened. "Mama—"

"I'm not asking, Sara. Go on."

Reluctantly, Sara clambered out of her bed and raced out of the room with Meliv at her heels. As soon as they were gone, Kamari relaxed a little, sinking against the bed and combing her fingers through Venni's hair.

"I can't let you and Xenah go alone," she said. "I don't trust him not to try things *his way* and—I mean no offense when I say this—but I don't believe you could stop him either. The fact is Sefah will kill him, or he will kill Sefah, and I don't like either of those outcomes. I have to go."

"Sefah doesn't want to fight." Tetsunah twisted the hem of her shirt, pulling until it wound around all five fingers. "But he will defend himself if attacked. He's… not himself. Something's wrong with him."

Kamari paused, a thoughtful frown overtaking her features. "Get dressed," she finally said. "We're leaving as soon as Rym arrives."

Tetsunah turned to leave, desperate to bury the tangled knot of uncertainty that was slowly growing in her chest. She made it to the door before a quiet voice caught her ear.

"Find Papa…" Venni whispered. "Make him c–come home, Mama." Hesitantly, a small smirk made its way to her lips, the perfect mirror of Xen's sly grin. Her playful confidence returned for a flickering moment. "Kick his butt," she added.

Xen. Tetsunah's lip twitched at his influence, knowing Kamari would be none too pleased. Despite that, however, Kamari gave a soft chuckle.

"I'll find him," she said. "He'll come home and make this right. I promise. Just hold on until then."

Choked by the thorns of regret that burrowed deep into her flesh, Tetsunah left the room and closed the door softly behind herself. *Tell Kamari I'm sorry,* Sefah had said. She knew better than most that it would take more than *sorry* to fix the damage he had caused.

VIII

Meliv tightened Kamari's breastplate while the silver dragonborn examined the Draconic script painted on her sword's sheath. Her thumb traced the letters, her gaze distant and dark. Pity rose up like weeds in Tetsunah's chest and choked the hope that had rooted itself within her. If she wasn't careful, it too would soon die.

It was a miracle Xen was still there. Rage burned in his eyes, and he refused to stop fidgeting with his sword. Up and down, it slid out of his sheath and back in. The scrape of metal grated against Tetsunah's ears, and she winced, flattening them down. "Xen," she said, "it's going to be alright. We'll find Sefah. Venni will be okay."

"I should have killed him when I had the chance," he growled. "Then this winter curse would be lifted and Venni wouldn't be suffering right now."

"If I may…" Meliv cleared her throat and straightened, stepping away from Kamari. She folded her hands in front of her and kept her head low. "If you kill Sefah, she would be suffering a different kind of pain."

The hilt of Xen's sword slammed against his sheath. Meliv

flinched. "What else are we supposed to do? There's no other way!"

"That's enough," Kamari snapped. She spun to face him, the tail of her long coat billowing out around her legs. She leveled him with a stern look.

Even though the look wasn't directed at Tetsunah, she straightened anyway and held her breath. There was nothing quite like a mother's stare—although Tetsunah had never had a mother herself, having been spoken into existence by the Being, the all-powerful creator of Anticuus. However, a solid glare, hardened with an unspoken warning, still managed to make her skin crawl. She could only imagine Xen felt the same, judging from the tension crackling between them.

His jaw twitched. With a growl, he jerked his chin up and turned away from her. "If you say so."

Kamari's stare remained for a heartbeat longer before she released a sigh, and the tension slowly ebbed from her shoulders. Lifting her arm, she beckoned the shadows lurking in the entrance to the hallway behind her. "Koen, Sara, come here please."

Tetsunah stiffened as two small figures emerged from the doorway. Sara clung to Koen's hand, her face streaked with tears and her curls still a tangled mess. Koen kept his head high, his shoulders straight. It did little to mask the trembling in his arms, but his expression was firm, and his grip on his sister was steady. As soon as they came near enough, Kamari knelt and scooped them into her arms, threading her fingers through Koen's coal black hair.

"Meliv is in charge until I return with your father. You are to give her space to take care of Venni. If you start to feel ill, you must tell her. Am I clear?" Kamari instructed, voice muffled against the two childrens' heads.

Sara answered first with a quick "yes, Mama" that quivered with the beginnings of another bout of tears. It took everything in Tetsunah to keep herself grounded in her place, to not wrap the small girl in her own arms and offer to stay with her while she cried. It wasn't fair. Nothing about their situation held a sliver of mercy for the children of Sefah. Even they were subject to winter's wrath.

"Bring Father home," Koen said, voice soft and a little bit hesitant. He pulled away from the hug. There was a deeper level of understanding in the way he held Kamari's gaze. Unlike Sara and Venni, who didn't quite grasp the truth of the situation, Koen seemed to know the weight of what was upon them.

Tetsunah looked away and fiddled with the gold trim of her cloak, now dry and draped over her once more. The scent of blood was completely scrubbed from it, as well as the discoloration it would have left behind. Meliv was strangely talented at removing the dark, crimson stains. Still, it brought little comfort, a fragile wall between her and the threat of Sefah's wrath that loomed over them. Her stomach twisted painfully and the taste of bile coated her tongue. She quickly swallowed it back down. *No, not Sefah,* she reminded herself, dragging up the memory of the pleading look in his eyes. *Winter. Winter has a hold on him.*

After a moment, Kamari let go of Sara and Koen, a shaky smile on her lips as she tucked Sara's hair behind her pointed ears. "It's going to be okay," she whispered. "Be good for Meliv. Koen, take care of your sisters."

"Of course." Koen returned her smile. As she rose to stand, he took Sara's hand again and gently guided her to Meliv's side. She stumbled after him in a daze, eyes watery and red. Sniffling, she wiped her nose and hid her face.

"Bring Papa home safely," Sara murmured. A hiccuping sob built up in her throat, and her tears spilled free once more. Meliv quickly scooped her up and, with an apologetic glance at Kamari, left the room.

Only Koen stayed, small beneath the brave face he put on.

Tetsunah twisted her cloak in her hands again and swallowed past the lump in her throat.

"We should go," Xen said. "We're wasting time. Sefah is waiting."

That time, Kamari kept silent, but the twitch in her jaw hinted to the retort she kept locked away behind gritted teeth. Ignoring Xen, she gathered Koen into her arms one last time, squeezing his shoulder.

"I'll be home soon. Everything's going to be okay," Kamari murmured. "Be safe and take care of each other while I'm gone."

"Yes, Mama," Koen's muffled voice replied. He relaxed into her embrace and buried his face in her arm. Only the tufts of his coal black hair were visible from where Tetsunah stood.

Tetsunah cleared her throat, tugging on the edge of her cloak again. "Kamari."

"Yes. Yes, I know." Kamari pulled away and pressed a quick kiss to Koen's head. When she rose again, she turned sharply on her heel and made straight for the door. She didn't look back as she snatched her white cloak from the stand. Cold wind whipped inside the moment she swung the door open, bitter and uninviting. Kamari stepped out into it, unflinching with her head held high.

Xen clapped Tetsunah on the back, sending her stumbling with a gasp. She whirled to face him and met with his usual beam of confidence. He walked past her steadily and proudly, as if his wound was never there. "Come on then, Tet. Don't want to keep Sefah waiting."

"Good luck," Koen called as Xen stepped out the door. "Take care of each other."

Another gust of wind whisked inside. Tetsunah stiffened, muscles tensing to keep from shivering, and buried her fingers deeper in her cloak. Though she was warmer back in her own clothes, her feet tucked safely away inside her brown boots, the air that came from the Aurora Range was cold enough that it cut right through her. She was mere inches from the doorway, inches from being smothered in the unforgiving icy tempest that raged outside. *Sefah needs me.* She exhaled a shuddering breath. *He needs me. I have to bring him back to his senses and free him from winter's control.*

Pushing her shoulders back, Tetsunah lifted her chin and stepped out. Her hand caught the door latch and she pulled it closed. Immediately, the fiery warmth vanished from her back, sealed inside the house along with the pale orange glow from the hearth. Her boots sank into the snow. The breeze snapped at her cheeks. Dark clouds obscured the sun's light, casting heavy shadows over the mountainside.

Sefah needs me. She pulled the neck of her cloak up to her chin. *My people need me. I can't let the cold stop me.*

Kamari swung her cloak over her shoulders, fumbling with the clasp. White fur filled out the neckline; the hem at the bottom was embroidered with tiny blue snowflakes. As soon as she situated it, she turned to Xen with a murderous look, pupils narrowed like slits. Snow crunched as she marched over to him. Her hand shot out from beneath her cloak and snagged his scarf, yanking him down to her height. "Xenah," she warned, "I've told you this before and I'll say it again: you do *not* talk that way in front of my kids, especially not about Sefah."

"Relax." Xenah pried her hands free and straightened. "I get it. I'll never say another word about violence in your house again."

"Is everything a joke to you?" she hissed, wrenching out of his grip.

"Only the funny things in life."

"This isn't the time for jokes, Xenah." Kamari seethed, her cheeks darkening a shade as her scales lit up with the faint glow of magic. With the sweep of her arm, she gestured to the distant Aurora Range behind her. "What part of this amuses you? That's your friend out there. He's killing innocent people, destroying the world with his ice, injuring you because you opposed him, and you think this is funny?"

Xen bristled, golden eyes flashing. "Of course not! I want to stop him just as much as you do, and believe me, I know what he's doing is wrong. I'm prepared to do whatever I must do to stop him in order to protect you, Tet, and everyone else. Even if that means I must kill him."

"*No!*" Kamari snapped. Loose flecks of magic crackled around her fingers, untethered by her will. They tainted the air with a pressure as dizzying as a growing storm. "No, there will be no killing. I'm going to bring *my* Sefah back. The one who tells bad jokes and over-explains them when no one laughs, who squints too hard because his eyesight is laughably poor, who treats others with kindness even when they don't do the same. That's not the man who hurt you or unleashed this storm or infected the people of Aire with the frostbite plague. The man I love—the real Sefah—is still out there somewhere, and we're going to bring him home *alive*, no matter what we must do. Do you understand?"

As he always did when Kamari opposed him, Xen gritted his teeth and jerked his gaze away. Something unreadable darkened his expression, and his fingers tapped impatiently against his arm. If Kamari was the storm, the ocean that thrashed against the shore and threatened to devour any who stood too close to its borders, Xen was the wind that ripped across the land and edged the storm on. Tetsunah pictured herself as nothing but a stray petal, caught between the two and struggling to regain control.

Another shiver wracked her body, her teeth chattering. She tucked further into her cloak. "Please," she whispered. "Please don't fight anymore. We have to work together if we want to stop this. Sefah needs us. He... He spoke with me."

Kamari hesitated. Her breath clouded when she exhaled,

white like the flecks of snow that caught in her black curls. "He *spoke* with you?"

"The amulet reached out to me. When I opened myself to it, he was there." Tetsunah shifted away, shrinking back under the weight of Kamari's stare. "Something's wrong with winter. He told me to stay away, but I know he's struggling. He needs our help. Killing him isn't the answer."

Confusion flickered across Xen's face, something dark lurking in the depths. "How do you know you can trust anything he said to you?"

"Because I know Sefah. You did too, once."

He narrowed his eyes. "You're being naive, Tet. He's not Sefah anymore. He's the lord of winter."

"No," Tetsunah bit back. "Let me try things my way first. Promise you won't do anything until I try what I know."

Xen's hesitation was more painful than his words. The distrust that lingered in his face cut her to the bone, almost as cold as the wind that whipped around them. Finally, he dipped his head in submission to her request. Tetsunah sighed in relief. "Thank you, Xen."

He said nothing, and the conversation ended.

Kamari walked away, boots crunching snow. "We've wasted enough time. Where's Rym?"

In response, Rym's deep, hollow roar boomed from behind the clouds seconds before his gold-orange body plunged through the dark gray covering. The flurries of ice melted as they brushed his scales, sizzling with the heat that rolled off him in waves. Sunlight broke through the hole in the clouds and glistened across his scales, illuminating him in a brilliant, amber light. His talons scraped the snow, wings fluttering at his sides as he slowly lowered himself to the ground. For such a large creature—nearly three times the size of a horse—he landed gracefully a few paces from where they stood. He snorted, expelling smoke from his nose.

"Rym!" Tetsunah hiked her skirt up and ran to the dragon's side. Her hand met his scales, flattening her palm against them. They were warm to the touch, and she sighed as his heat dispelled the chill in her bones. She tilted her head back to gaze up at his elegantly curved face, his twisted horns jutting out from his forehead like a crown. "It's good to see you," she said, beaming at him.

Kamari drifted to the dragon, hand outstretched to touch his side as well. "Impressive that he could make it back so quickly."

"He can't stay here long. It's too cold for him," Xen explained. "However, he promised to get us to the Aurora Range."

The sun dragon lowered his head with a faint hum. His large snout brushed Tetsunah's shoulder, warm breath fanning her face. Wide, intelligent yellow eyes stared back at her, the echo of a flame burning in their depths. The light seemed duller than it used to be, darkened with melancholy. She smoothed a hand across his scales as a flicker of grief bloomed within her like a patch of weeds. "I wish Dei was here," she murmured.

Being the spirit of summer, she had an affinity for fire—wild and bright, just like her. She was exceptionally skilled at wielding it, though she had always struggled to control it and chose a life of solitude to protect those around her from her power. Although the level of her power was still below Sefah's, flames were a natural combatant to ice. She would have been able to stand a chance against him if he attacked again. Moreover, she would have known what to say to him. *But she's gone.* Tetsunah couldn't help but picture the amulet: the darkness in Deiah's summer rune, the void created by her absence. Though part of her lived on through the summer cycle, Deiah herself— the person, Tetsunah's friend—was gone.

"I miss her, too." Xen came and stood beside Tetsunah, looking up at Rym. "We can't stay stuck in the past. It's our duty to move toward the future, to continue to protect and watch over this world. That's what Dei would want. That's what we must do."

Rym slowly dipped his head in a nod, yellow eyes closing as he sighed another plume of smoke. He lowered himself to the ground, his belly pressing against the snow, and allowed them to climb onto his back. Xenah lifted Tetsunah, and she hauled herself onto the dragon, gripping his warm, amber scales until her knuckles ached. Kamari and Xen climbed up behind her. Even with three people on his back, Rym rose easily to his full height, and Tetsunah guessed there was still room for a fourth person behind Kamari if they squished together. With a powerful leap, Rym pushed off the ground and soared into the air, angling himself toward the distant Aurora Range and its white-tipped peaks.

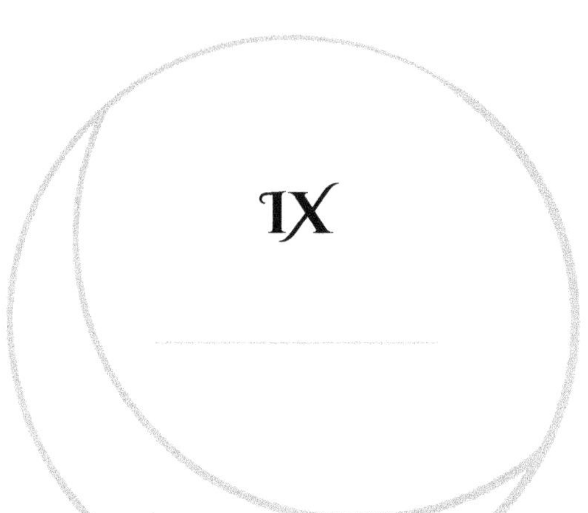

IX

In contrast to the plains of Aire and even to the mountainside where Kamari's home was, the Aurora Range was calm. Smoky clouds still blotted out the sun, but the air was stale. Wind and hail ravaged the land beyond, but the storm didn't touch the mountain's peaks. It was the eye of the storm: the safe haven at the center of the destruction. However, being the central part of Sefah's realm, it was still frigid enough to chill Tetsunah to the bone. The ground remained blanketed in a thick layer of snow. Rym's legs sank into it, swallowed halfway up before it began to melt from the heat that rolled off his scales. Displeased, he snorted and drew back, his lip curling. His tail lashed across the ground and sent chunks of powder flying through the air.

Tetsunah slipped from his back and tumbled into the snow-drift. Bitter, wet cold sank its claws into her skin. She tensed against it and gasped. During the ride, she had grown accustomed to Rym's sun-soaked scales. Now, thrust back into the snow, she winced at the loss of the warmth. Xen's arm hooked underneath hers and hauled her back to her feet. "Thanks," she muttered as he released her.

Kamari jumped down last, giving Rym's neck a soft pat. In her white gloves and white cloak, she almost blended entirely into the mountain. "Thank you for getting us this far," she said. She tilted her head back to meet Rym's watchful eye. "We'll be fine here."

"Go on, friend." Xen waved a dismissive hand at the dragon. "Find someplace warm to wait for my signal. You've earned it." He stopped, face contorting as if something had occurred to him, then added in a grumble, "If there's a warm place left anymore."

Rym studied them for a moment, eyes flicking from face to face. A hesitant hum rumbled in the back of his throat as he lowered his head, brushing his snout against Kamari's shoulder. Leaning in, Kamari tilted her head so that her horns touched his scales, her hands tucked against his chin. She spoke a few words of Draconic, shared only between the two of them, before she pulled away. The moment her touch left him, Rym lifted his head and stretched his wings. With a final snort, he bounded away and pushed himself into the air. His orange-and-gold body vanished behind the cover of ominous gray clouds. In his absence, the penetrating chill crept in once more, its ghostly whispers trailing cold fingers down Tetsunah's spine. She stiffened and pulled her cloak tighter.

Kamari breathed a deep, shuddering breath and wrapped her arms around herself as she tucked her chin into the fur-lined collar of her coat. "Come on. We still have a lot of ground to cover if we want to find Sefah, and I'd prefer to do that before nightfall. There's not much sun now due to the storm, but I don't want to be here when it's gone completely."

"He has a camp out here, right?" Tetsunah asked. She sifted through her memories for a thread that might lead them to his location, but she could only come up with the vague image of a modest camp tucked in an alcove against the side of the rocky, snow-covered cliffs. Usually, Sefah left the mountains to meet with the other spirits, saying he didn't want them to be uncomfortable in his realm. She had only been to the Aurora Range once before, but it all looked the same in her memories. It didn't help that as the cold numbed her body, it began to slur her thoughts as well.

Xen frowned, humming in thought as he did a full turn to survey the area. Rym had dropped them off on the flat stretch of land between the two largest peaks. The edge of the cliff was several miles from where they stood, but Tetsunah could see the drop-off clearly against the gray sky. There was nothing but rocks and snow. Tetsunah's eyes ached from staring at so much white; she yearned for a tree or two to break apart the constant oneness of the landscape, but those would never survive in the climate of the Aurora Range. Even she could feel what little ounce of magic she had beginning to shrivel away again.

"I think it's that way." Xen pointed to the taller peak north of their current position. A faint blue glow encircled the tip of the mountain, visible even at a distance. "Even if that's not where the camp is, Sefah has been there recently."

"Then that's where we'll go." Kamari trudged past him, shoulders hunched and head tucked low into the neckline of her cloak. The sword at her waist stuck out awkwardly beneath the white folds, shifting with each jagged, halting step. Her boots crushed ice, producing a satisfying *crunch* each time she took a step.

Tetsunah hauled her foot out of the almost-knee deep snow and followed the dragonborn. Redness darkened the tips of her fingers, and they had long since gone numb. She tucked her hands under her arms and shivered.

One step at a time. She stumbled. The snow was thick, her limbs frozen stiff.

One foot in front of the other. Her lungs ached from breathing in short, tight breaths. A sudden gust of wind buffeted against her, threatening to tear her cloak from her shoulders. Quickly, she grabbed the gold-embroidered edges and clung to them.

She was the spirit of spring; she lived to dispel the winter, yet she was trapped in its jaws, waiting to be swallowed whole by the beast that it was. Its teeth tore her flesh to bits until she was certain her blood would stain the pearly white snow a dark crimson. Its breath was the wind that nearly knocked her off her feet. It was a creature she could not tame, not without the help from its master. Yet he, too, was caged by the unruly monster.

Sefah's cold eyes flashed into her mind, narrowed and sharp. The snowflake rune in his left eye glowed so brightly she almost couldn't see the ultramarine of his iris beneath it. Frost crystallized on his fingers, turning his bronze skin white and blue. His thin lips were set in a careful frown, a different kind of vicious from the open-mouthed snarl of winter.

To tame the heart of winter, one must first calm the master. To calm the master, one must first set him free of the beast.

Tetsunah glanced down, lifting her hand from the folds of her cloak. It trembled with the cold, her pale skin red and aching. Faint sparks of pink gathered at the tips, swirling and dancing with the familiar pull of magic. It crawled beneath her skin, taking refuge within the core of her being. It was only a trickling stream, the barest speck of life, but it was there. Curling her fingers into a fist, she dropped it back to her side.

She was Tetsunah, the spirit of spring. It was her duty to dispel winter, to quell its wrath and put it to sleep until time came for it to rise again. If there was anyone who should be able to silence its wrath, it was her.

I'm sorry, Sefah, but I can't wait any longer for you to wrestle your control. Too many had died already. Too much was at stake to wait on his pride. If she had even the slightest chance at righting his wrongs, she had to take it. For Aire, for Erix, for Venni, and for Sefah himself.

Shaky confidence began to build up her resolve. Fueled by it, her spine straightened, her steps growing more sure. She lifted her chin to face the mountaintop that loomed over her. Its azure crown of magic quivered, spinning the image of a tyrant that sneered as it waited to deliver punishment upon her. *You have no power*, she reminded the mountain, clenching her jaw. *The spell will be broken, and the wrath of winter will end.*

The mountain didn't flinch at her words.

Kamari, however, came to a sudden stop, a gasp snatched from her lips. She thrust her arm out in front of Tetsunah, her body angled toward something away from the rocky cliffs that stood over them. As soon as Tetsunah came to a stop, Kamari wrenched her arm away and put her hand against the hilt of her sword. "Where's Xenah?"

A fresh wave of fear slammed into Tetsunah's fragile wall of courage, cracking it. She spun, jaw tight and eyes wide. He had vanished from behind her, his form nowhere in sight. His red scarf and yellow coat should have been easy to spot against the snow, and yet there was nothing. "Xenah?" she called. "Xen!"

"He is here."

Both Kamari and Tetsunah turned to face the voice. Sefah stood a few paces away, his back to the peak they were headed toward. Its icy crown haloed him in a blue glow, softer than the moon's light had been before, but it didn't remove the hardness in his gaze. His face was uncovered this time, the wrap draped over one shoulder and tucked into his belt. Unlike when she spoke with him in the amulet, he seemed cold and collected—cruel almost, as the white rune's glow had completely overtaken his eye. In one hand, he clutched Xenah's maroon scarf, twisting it around his fist so that it pulled up against Xen's neck. A slim blade of ice rested against the exposed skin of his neck while a dark blue thread of Sefah's magic bound Xen's hands together. Despite every-thing, Xen remained relaxed, his golden-amber eyes flicking from Tetsunah to Sefah. He tilted his chin slightly, the corners of his mouth twitching up. Sefah tightened his grip on the scarf.

"I asked you to stay away," he growled. "I have everything under control, and yet you disregarded my concern and brought Xen here to kill me?"

"Well, technically, I haven't tried anything *yet*." Xen shrugged.

The ice-knife dug into his neck and drew blood. His breath hitched, and he fell silent.

Sefah pulled back on the scarf. "Your arrogance is your weakness, Xenah. You would do well not to press."

"Sefah!" Tetsunah shoved her way forward, brushing past Kamari's protective arm and marching through the thick snow. His gaze swiveled to her, piercing and *wrong*; the snowflake rune flashed. She swallowed hard and pressed on. "Let him go. He hasn't done anything wrong."

"He opposes my divine right." The words came out flat, almost automatic. They were void of Sefah's inflection. *As if they came from somewhere else.*

"Talk to me, Sefah." Tetsunah raised her hands and slowed her pace, approaching him calmly as one might a wild animal. Only a few feet separated them now. "We talked before, remember? It was just a few hours ago. You told me you didn't want to hurt any of us. You told me there was something wrong with winter."

"Tetsunah!" Kamari cried, snow crunching as she took a step forward.

Tetsunah threw out a hand to stop her but did not remove her focus from Sefah's face. Her body buzzed, alight with nervous energy that fluttered like a bird in a cage, eager to break free. *One step after another; one foot in front of the other.* Slowly, she came closer.

Sefah hesitated. Something flickered in his expression,

wavering for just a moment. His grip slackened, and the ice knife lowered from Xenah's neck.

The moment Sefah lowered his guard, Xen's smile burst to life on his face. He chuckled. Lifting his arms, he snapped his wrists free of the thread and summoned his sword. He twisted free, leaving his scarf behind in Sefah's outstretched hand, and spun to face him, lifting the blade against his neck. "Did you think your little tricks could best me? You've truly become a fool, Sefah."

A terrifying mix of panic and anger burst to life beneath the surface of Tetsunah's skin. Magic raced to her grasp, spurred on by the sudden storm of emotion. She grasped the faint thread and clung tightly to it, winding it around her fingers, careful not to let it slip away. "Xen, don't!" she cried.

Her legs moved of their own accord; she shot forward, dropping her cloak in the snow, and grasped Sefah by the arm. With a fierce tug, she pulled him below the arc of Xen's sword as he took a swing. They tumbled to the ground, their fall cushioned by the thick build-up of powder. Wet, frigid cold sank through Tetsunah's dress, and her breath hitched. Sefah shoved upright, his eyes wide like a frightened animal. When they finally met hers, his gaze softened.

"Tetsunah, you..." He faltered, lips parting but no words came out.

Blades clashed overhead, ringing with the sharp clang of metal on metal. Kamari's silver sword pushed back against Xen's, shielding Sefah and Tetsunah from the autumn spirit's rage. With a roar, Kamari shoved him back. Xenah stumbled and lost his footing, collapsing in the snow.

"Tetsunah, whatever it is you plan to do, now is your chance." She gave a firm nod, her gaze lingering on Sefah for a moment before she turned back to Xen as he rose shakily to his feet. "I'll keep this *desika* busy."

She lunged for Xen, sword raised, and they clashed again.

Sefah watched in a daze, brow furrowed and uncertain. "Kamari," he murmured as he brought a hand to his temples.

"Sefah, something is distorting your thoughts." Tetsunah crawled forward, ignoring the numbing cold crawling up her legs. She placed a hand on either side of his head—red fingers stark against his white hair—and pulled on the droplet of magic left in her core. A pink glow enveloped her palms, warm against her skin. "Relax your mind and let me heal you."

He tensed at first, focus shifting to her face as the snowflake rune in his left eye brightened. Slowly, the glow dulled and his shoulders began to droop. The tension fled from him, and his body sagged forward as he exhaled a sigh of relief. As he did, the piercing air lessened its bite ever so slightly.

Exhaustion began to creep into Tetsunah's limbs as her magic dried up, but the look in Sefah's eyes was still distant. She bowed her head and let her eyes flutter shut. A single pink thread wound through the recesses of her mind, flowing and winding like a river. It stretched out from her to someplace far away, the end unseen in her mind's eye, but she knew it connected to Erix back home in Aire. She could feel his presence on the other end, faint as it was. Pinching her lips, she grasped the thread. *Sorry, my friend.* She tugged on it, letting some of the power she had lent him flow back into her, which she then poured into her spell. Purification. Healing. Calming. These were things she could do; this was what being the spirit of spring was about.

"Stop."

Cold hands gripped hers, icy nails digging into her skin. Frost bloomed across her wrists, freezing the flow of magic beneath the surface. Her eyes snapped open, immediately falling upon his. Unending ultramarine depths gazed back at her, glistening with fear. The white snowflake rune stamped onto his left eye wavered for a moment, flickering in and out of focus. Sefah's grip tightened as his frown deepened.

"You can't stay here," he said, his voice like the whisper of wind as it caressed her cheek. "I can't let you interfere."

She stiffened. Unease squirmed within her. "Sefah—"

"Sleep," he whispered, dragging a hand down her face. A faint blue light formed at the tips of his frost-covered fingers, brighter than anything else in view.

Heaviness overcame her and she slumped forward, dimly aware of his arms supporting her. A ringing filled her ears; it drowned out the sound of someone's shout. Her eyes closed of their own accord, and the world fell away into darkness.

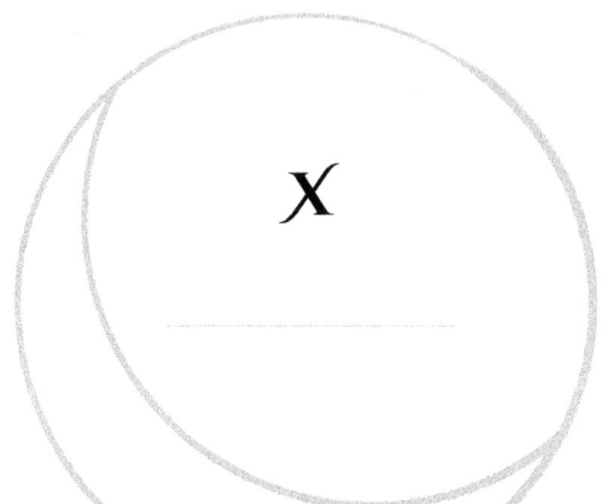

X

Sharp ringing penetrated Tetsunah's ears. Her mind was a bog, her thoughts forced to wade through a thick, muddy swamp before they could arrive at a solid conclusion. Slowly, the threads of consciousness wove themselves back together, and she groaned softly. Hard stone pressed against her body. She shifted, lifting herself upright and dragging a hand to her temples. Cold metal dug into her wrists; chains rattled and pulled taut against her, stopping her before her fingers even brushed her forehead. Her eyes snapped open, gaze jerking down to the chains that bound her. Pure ice stared back at her, not metal. It glittered with the aura of Sefah's magic.

"I'm sorry, Tetsunah, but it was the only way to stop you."

Her breath hitched as she swiveled toward the source of the voice. Sefah stood in the mouth of the cave, blue flecks of magic twirling around his fingers. His back faced her as he cast a spell over the opening to the alcove. Snow and wind raged outside, but it was strangely warm in the cave—or at least warmer than it had been outside. Tetsunah could still feel the crushing bite of winter beneath her skin.

"Sefah," she murmured. Grogginess clung to her, sapping the strength from her voice. She shifted again, her back against the rocky wall directly opposite the opening. She was sitting against it, her legs tucked up under her skirt and her arms both clamped in ice chains. Her cloak was gone, sparking a flicker of panicked fear in her chest before the memory of dropping it surfaced. Shivering, she tucked closer to the wall. "Where are Kamari and Xen?"

As he finished, Sefah lowered his hand and turned to her. A thin shield hung over the entrance, similar to the barrier that barred the tunnel beneath Aire. In place of the flowering rune of spring, there was the fragile image of a snowflake, a mirror to the one in Sefah's left eye. His lips curled up in a tiny smile, heavy with sadness.

"I know you came to help, but I wish you had listened to me," he said softly. "I was trying to keep you safe."

His dismissal of her question set off the fluttering nerves in her chest. "You still can't control it, can you?" she murmured, brow furrowing as a frown creased her lips. "That was... winter back there, wasn't it?"

"Xen attacked me. I had to fight back." He looked away, breathing a soft sigh as he lifted a hand to touch his cheek below his left eye. Delicate swirls of frost bloomed across his dark skin. "I'm sorry. I needed to speak with you privately. There's something I couldn't say before." A pause stretched between his words as his gaze swept over her. Realization settled in his gaze, and he waved his hand. The chains dissolved immediately. "Sorry. Your magic was leaking out, and I wasn't sure what sort of state you would be in when you awoke."

The moment the harsh binds dropped away, Tetsunah rubbed away the ache in her wrists. She shifted and pushed to her feet. Her legs trembled beneath her, weak like a newborn fawn, and she leaned against the wall for support. "Kamari's worried about you. You should be talking to her. In fact, you should be going back to her right now because—"

"I had a vision."

Tetsunah's argument came to a screeching halt, her tongue dry and stuck to the roof of her mouth. She swallowed hard. "A vision?" she echoed.

"Of the truth and the future." He stepped closer, sweeping his scarf over his shoulder. "Our people slaughtered, the kingdom of Calistie in ruins, Selini's soldiers marching into our home." He leveled his gaze with her. Sadness darkened his eyes. "War is coming, Tetsunah. Fear destroyed my control. I was weak, and now, everyone is suffering because of me."

Horror seized Tetsunah's lungs, squeezing the breath out of them until her vision flickered black. "War?" The word came out as barely more than a squeak, pitiful and weak in the face of the image he painted for her. She could see it in the back of her mind, her home and people destroyed by the dragon goddess.

Being forbidden to cross into Draconic territory, she had seen very few dragonborn in her lifetime, but their brutality was known across the land. They were a proud people, toting the title of *perfection* with them wherever they went as if it was their divine right in their goddess. Filled with power and strength, they tormented the humans and elves with relentless, violent attacks in the dead of night. She had seen the carnage left in their wake—bodies torn apart, blood spattered across the ground, glassy, unfocused eyes open and staring emptily above. Yet the Draconic people had never marched with the intent to ravage an entire kingdom, only to hunt and kill in small groups like a pack of wolves. It was unheard of, but the resolve—the truth—in Sefah's gaze was clear as day.

"Do you understand?" Sefah turned and paced away from her, raking his fingers through his thin, snow-white hair. As he moved, she could feel the chill rolling off him in waves. "I can't let that happen to our people. I don't know what to tell Kamari.

I don't know how to show my face again after what I've done. I'm a fool, Tet. A coward and a fool." He stopped, gritting his teeth as he pressed his fists to his eyes and sucked in a sharp breath. "Everyone was right about me. I'm a monster."

"No." Tetsunah shoved away from the wall and stumbled to him, taking his hands. "No, we can fix this. I don't know about your vision, but we can rein winter back under your control," she whispered, searching his face. His usual softness had returned, and the empty look of the white snowflake was gone. His eyes glistened with unshed tears, giving him a fragile appearance, one that reminded her of the glass unicorn she had cradled in his home. *And yet...* The winter storm raged outside. The frostbite sickness no doubt still ate away at her people back in Aire. Despite his softness, the pitiful look in his brilliant blue eyes, the cold season he wielded was still part of him. No matter how much he denied it, some part of him was still stirred in rage. Seasons didn't simply become *uncontrollable.* The spirits were created to wield them, to lead them, to control them. They were extensions of their wills.

Intended or not, part of Sefah had unleashed the wrath of winter to punish Anticuus for his vision.

She pressed her lips into a thin line and lowered her head, her bangs falling in her face. "Venni is sick," she said. "She... has the frostbite plague."

"Venni." The coat of frost on his fingers thickened, biting into Tetsunah's red-kissed hands. She gasped and snapped them back. When she lifted her gaze, she saw the wide look of panic in his eyes. His breaths came in short gasps. Pursing his lips, he grabbed her shoulders and held tight. "Is this true?"

She nodded slowly as her vision blurred with tears, her throat constricting painfully. "That's why we have to stop this. She can't wait for you to wrestle with winter, Sefah. Young children never make it long once the sickness takes hold of them."

His long, pointed ears drooped as the weight of the truth

settled on his shoulders. Not even his own family was safe from the wrath of winter; time was too short for him to fight on his own. The white rune flickered, growing brighter again. Tetsunah put her hand against his arm and let her magic flow into him. It tugged at her core as a warmth settled in the tips of her fingers, glowing pink with magic's touch. As soon as the healing power began to seep into him, the rune calmed once more, and he took a shaky breath.

"I'm here," she said. "I won't let winter control your mind anymore."

He dipped his head and let his hands fall back to his sides, silent as a ghost.

Tetsunah released him. "How do we stop it? How do we end the plague and the storm?"

Sefah began to pace again, flurries of snow drifting through the air around him. His shoulders trembled, arms folded over his chest. When he exhaled, his breath clouded in front of him, glowing blue from his magic. "If we had more time, I could do it myself. I just need more time."

"We don't have that much to spare, Sefah." Tetsunah's fingers bunched up her skirt, pressing the fabric against her palms. Cold gripped her chest, edged with fear. Aire didn't have time to spare, it never had, and yet the urgency she saw in Sefah was new. He saw the destruction in Sheniir, he knew he needed to gain control and calm winter once more, but there was nothing quite like his love for his family to light a fire beneath him. She just hoped he could figure it out before the flames consumed him.

Suddenly, he stopped, his head snapping up as his gaze settled emptily ahead. Frantically, he turned to her, boots scuffing against the stone. "If we had all four spirits here, I know a way for us to stop this. But..." Sadness darkened his ultramarine eyes, and he looked away. "Dei is gone. We can't do it without all of us present."

The bitter tang of guilt coated Tetsunah's tongue. She could still remember the moment darkness overtook the summer rune. They all knew she was gone, though the grief had never properly set in for Tetsunah, leaving her painfully numb instead. Her hands were full with her duties as a Seasonal Spirit, and when the frostbite plague swept in, she barely even had a moment to breathe, much less offer anything more than a wistful longing for Dei. And now, they would pay the price for her absence. Tears welled in her eyes, and she fiercely blinked them away. "Is there truly no other way?"

Sefah went stiff. He pressed a fist to his lips and flicked his gaze away. "I—I can condense the wrath and put it all into a single being, like a curse. However, there's a catch: it can't be myself, it must be a living being, and it must be someone that possesses strong magic." His jaw tightened and he let the silence stand for a moment before he finally spoke again. "I won't subject anyone to that kind of curse. I've already taken too many lives."

As soon as he mentioned it, a new possibility opened up before Tetsunah. Hope bloomed within her; it was a small blossom, its petals barely beginning to unfold as it rose slowly from the depths, but it was enough. She cradled it close to her chest as her confidence strengthened. Setting her jaw, she met Sefah's eye with an even and determined look.

"Give it to me," she said. "I'm the spirit of spring. It's my duty to help you end winter."

He flinched as if struck, but the look in his eyes turned fierce and icy. "It will kill you, Tet. I can't do that."

"Would you give it to Xen? Or Kamari?"

"No!"

"Then you would wait and watch Venni die along with countless others?"

"I can't let you die for my mistakes." Tendrils of frost climbed slowly up his arm and touched the edge of his long sleeve. Though he had never been one to mind the cold, his whole body was trembling now. Fear had seized him, evident in the tears welling in his eyes and the way his thin lips quivered. The lines in his face contorted his expression into something hollow, made eerie by the shadows that hung over him. He had never been so fragile. The sight pricked Tetsunah's nerves and gave way to the thorny vines of anger within her.

"So you're going to let pride control you?" Tetsunah tightened her fists until her nails dug into her skin. "I'm offering a solution, the only one we know will work right now, and you won't even consider it?"

"Because I care about you, Tetsunah!" he snapped, swiping at the air. The flurries of snow morphed into tiny spikes of ice, hovering around him with their tips aimed at Tetsunah. "I'm not sacrificing you. You're my friend!"

"Did you stop to think about your family?" she bit back. "You didn't tell Kamari about your vision—you didn't even say goodbye to her when you left! You didn't think to ask me or Xen for help when this started. You ran away and cursed everyone else to deal with your rage while you struggled to find yourself again!"

He narrowed his eyes, the white rune flashing again. His clarity remained, but the light was enough to make Tetsunah step back. "What point are you trying to make?"

Warily, Tetsunah glanced between him and the small flecks of ice around them. Her heartbeat thundered in her ears; she was almost certain he could hear it echoing off the cave walls, too. *He's not a threat to you,* she reminded herself. *You cleared his mind. He's upset, naturally. Calm. Remind him you're not a threat either.* Taking a deep breath, she exhaled the tension that gathered in her muscles. "Let us help you, Sefah. Let me take this burden from you, please. I don't want to see you suffer any longer."

As if knocked away by an invisible force, the spikes of ice

surrounding him dropped. They shattered against the stone, throwing tiny bits at their feet before dissolving in a shower of blue sparks. His shoulders went slack, and he dragged a hand across his face as he stepped toward her. "There's no coming back," he warned, searching her face. "Are you sure you want to do this?"

"I am." She didn't hesitate for even a moment, certain to keep her expression firm. The moment he spotted even a hint of the fear that crawled beneath the surface, she knew he would deny her the chance. That was a risk she couldn't afford to take. If this was the only way to save her people, her friends, her *family*, she would take it.

Gentle as the first brush of snow, Sefah took her hands and cradled them in both of his. Her pale skin looked white as snow against his darker shade covered in webs of frost like a collection of scars. His eyes closed, and he bowed his head. Ice crystallized on her skin, snuffing out the magic she had gathered in an instant. Bone-chilling cold settled over her as the ice worked its way under her skin. She snatched her hand back with a gasp, cradling it against her chest. Cracks split her flesh as the tips of her fingers slowly turned blue. *Like the frostbite plague.*

"I'm sorry," he whispered. She snapped her gaze back to him to find pity swirling in the depths of his eyes. He tried to smile, but it faltered and fell away the instant he dragged it up. "It is a curse, after all. It's going to be unpleasant."

Shivers wracked her body, and she sank to the ground. Blood roared in her ears as she curled in on herself. The ice crawled up her arm, sharper than any knife, digging into her skin. Winter's bite was something she had experienced before, but she never imagined ice could be so cold; it sapped her body of warmth, robbing it of strength. The pool of magic within her dried up, frozen over by the ice as it worked its way toward her heart. Agony tore through her body like thousands of nails driven into her. She stifled the cry that rose to her lips and buried her head in her trembling arms.

"Sefah," she rasped. "It's going to be okay." The words were broken by the tremors that shook her, teeth chattering against the chill. She squeezed her eyes shut, her tears frozen in place. She curled her fingers in her hair. They were already encased in ice. "Look after Aire for me."

"Goodbye, my friend."

In the next instant, the blue shield over the cave mouth shattered into thousands of tiny shards that dissolved in the air. Kamari and Xen stood behind it, weapons in hand, Xen's eyes alight with gold magic. It swirled around him in erratic, aggravated motions before frantically withdrawing back into him. He kept one arm wrapped around his midsection, and his breaths came in ragged gasps. Kamari, however, was in peak shape, quivering with rage. She raised her silver sword and pointed it at Sefah.

"Kamari," he breathed. He shuffled back and thrust his arm out in front of Tetsunah.

"Sefah." The name came out in a growl. Kamari narrowed her eyes. "Let Tetsunah go."

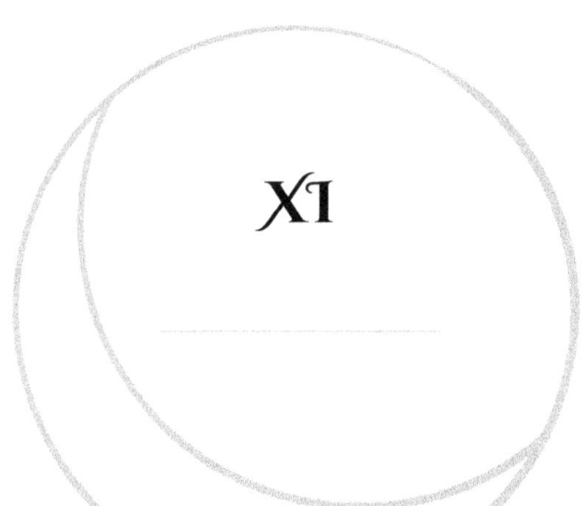

XI

Ice was consuming Tetsunah from the inside out. Her heart thundered in her chest, roaring in her ears. Panic drowned out the sound of Kamari and Sefah's voices, though they were mere feet away from her. Tremors seized her; no matter how hard she tried, she could not keep her body from shaking. A whimper escaped her, and she squeezed her eyes shut to avoid the sight of her skin, split apart by crystals of ice and tainted blue as the chill worked its way through her.

If this was what her people had suffered all this time, it was no wonder she had been powerless to stop it. As it consumed her life, sapped her strength, and drained her magic, she stood no chance against it now. Not that stopping it would do any good. She had only to let it take hold of her and vanish from the world. That was how she would calm the wrath of winter.

It hurts, her mind cried, screaming in her head though her lips were sealed shut. Bit by bit, her resolve crumbled, crushed beneath the force of the ice. *I wish there was another way. Make it stop.*

But Sefah couldn't hear her. Kamari held his attention now; Tetsunah could only hope she would be able to understand what they had done, and that she wouldn't try to stop him—though part of her wished she would. Agony ripped through her, and the conflict raged within her again. To suffer, bear the pain for the world, or be free and find another way.

"Tetsunah!" Xen's steady hand slid under her shoulder and lifted her from the rocky ground beneath her. Something thick wrapped around her shoulders, enveloping her in the scent of lavender—her cloak. His palm was warm when he pressed it to her forehead. "Stay with me, Tet. It's going to be okay. We'll get you out of here." The crack in his voice betrayed his fear. Even without asking, she knew he was aware of how pointless it was. There was no cure to the frostbite plague, no end to the wrath of winter. With a growl, he shot a searing glare at Sefah. "What did you do to her?"

Sefah raised his hands and stepped back, body tense as if he expected Xen to lunge at him and tear his throat out. "I transferred the wrath of winter to her. It's the only way to quell the storm and get rid of the plague in enough time to save Venni."

Xen's breath hitched at the mention of Venni. Even Kamari froze, her lips pinched with uncertainty. "Was there no other way?" she asked.

"It would take too long for me to undo what has been done myself, and Deiah isn't here so we can't perform the ceremony as spirits to stop it." Sefah's attention settled on Tetsunah, that pity once again welling in his eyes. "The only solution was to condense it into a curse and place it on a living being. Tet volunteered... to save our family."

"Take it off!" Xen roared, his arms tightening around Tetsunah. "Give it to me instead. You'll kill her!"

Sefah's gaze softened. "It would kill you, too."

"Fine by me," Xen spat. "I'd give my life to protect her. It hurts to know you can't say the same."

"Xenah." Kamari shook her head. Slowly, she slid her sword back into its sheath and approached Sefah. The tips of her fingers brushed his hand, warm olive against white-dusted bronze. "There must be another way. Please, love, you must know something."

"The only other way would be to give it to someone else."

Tetsunah squeezed her eyes shut as a fresh wave of pain rolled over her. *Or to kill him,* the traitorous part of her mind whispered, recalling the blinding fury in Xen's face, the unshakable resolve he had that drove him to take his sword against their friend.

There's no way to know that killing him would end the wrath of winter, she argued numbly. *His body is flesh, but his soul is winter itself. His magic is the heart of it. Perhaps killing him in this state would leave winter untethered, uncontrollable, and wild—more so than it already is.*

Her eyes fluttered open, tongue brushing her lips as she parted them. She turned her head toward Xen, her gaze landing on his. But the words turned to ice, a lump in her throat that refused to take the shape of her voice. She swallowed hard against it as icy tears slid down her cheeks.

A fragile, half-hearted smile curved his lips. He brushed her bangs out of her eyes. The usual confidence and cockiness in his face was gone, leaving behind the look of a small, frightened boy. His golden eyes were wide, dulled with pain and weakened from his pull on his magic. "It–it's going to be okay, Tet. I'm here. I promise, I'm here. We can fix this. We'll think of something else. Just stay with me, okay?"

She shook her head slowly, her lips quivering as she pinched them together. If there was anyone that knew, it was her: there was only so long she could hold on when winter was dragging her down. All things must die in winter, for spring is the rebirth. It was the natural cycle. She was simply the crux of it now.

Xen was not deterred. Determination and perseverance were some of his most admirable qualities, despite how stubborn they made him. A golden light emitted from his palm and traced swirling lines in her skin as it settled over her. It kissed her with soft warmth but could do little more than that. Like the faint rays of sunlight that dappled the forest ground, it could not melt the frost that clung to the shadows, and she found herself drenched in them.

Behind him, Kamari's white cloak swished as she moved, tapping her foot anxiously against the stone. Pale light glinted off her silver scales and horns, illuminating her like a star. Dragonborn hated to wait, legends said. They craved action, the ability to do something to change their situation. They were hardly ever left standing still for long. Despite the ice consuming her, Tetsunah found herself pitying Kamari.

"I'll do it," the dragonborn woman said, determination giving her the strength to stand up straighter under Sefah's incredulous gaze. "Give the curse to me. Let Tetsunah go."

"No." Sefah took her hands, threading his fingers between hers. Lips quivering, she leaned into him, resting her head against his shoulder. "I can't do that to you," he whispered. His next words came in a rush of Draconic, spoken less elegantly than Kamari but still quite fluently. Tetsunah wasn't even sure when he had learned.

"No, no, *no*." Xen's hand withdrew, snapping Tetsunah's focus back to him. His brow creased, his eyes wide with panic. They glistened with tears, something she couldn't recall having ever seen in his face. "It's not working," he breathed. "Nothing works. I can't stop it."

Tetsunah lifted her hand shakily. Ice encased it entirely, having made its way up past her elbow. She could feel the same in her toes, and the tightness in her chest sealed her fate. It was accelerating rapidly. Death would claim her in a matter of minutes.

Xen slid his arms around her shoulders, squeezing her against his chest. He tucked his chin against her head. She could feel his body shaking against hers. "It's useless. I'm not strong enough to break the spell."

"It's…" Tetsunah clenched her jaw, grinding her teeth against the tension in her skin. "Okay… I know there's n-nothing to be done." The words came out stilted, forced. To try to lessen their painful edge, she forced a weak smile. "Xen… please don't blame yourself. I asked for this. To save you."

Xen broke away from the embrace. Faint trails of tears stained his tanned skin, and the circles beneath his eyes were heavy with weariness. Still, his lips formed a thin line as determination sparked in his eyes. He twisted to face Sefah and Kamari, still locked in a battle behind him.

"Is this what you want, Sefah?" Xen called. Slowly, he shifted and laid Tetsunah gently against the stone. As he stood, a gasp pulled from his lips, and he stumbled, his shoulder slamming into the rocky wall.

His wound, Tetsunah realized with a jolt, but she could no longer move her limbs. She could no longer support him.

Xen pushed away from the wall and steadied himself. He faced Sefah fully now, who had broken away from Kamari and looked on with a pitiful guilt in his eyes. "You would sacrifice her life to fix *your* mess? I looked up to you. *Tet* looked up to you. You think *this* is going to wash your hands clean of this sin?" Xen spat. He summoned his sword and shifted his feet, dropping into an attack-ready stance. "I propose an alternative solution: a duel. If I win, I'm going to kill you and end this my way—"

"Xenah!" Kamari jerked away from Sefah and started to march toward Xen, her pale eyes blazing with fury. Sefah calmly stopped her with his hand on her shoulder. When she spun to face him, he only shook his head.

"—if you win, you will remove the curse from Tetsunah and place it on me. I will die to save your skin, Tet won't have to suffer, and you can go back to your family." Xen gripped his sword tighter. "Do we have a deal?"

Sefah's resolve cracked, his patient mask breaking away. It revealed itself in the twitch of his ears, the darkening of the white rune in his eye, the way his thin lips pressed themselves into a fragile line. Threads of magic formed at the tips of his fingers, weaving themselves into the shape of a sword made of pure ice. "Yes. We have a deal. I will remove the curse from Tetsunah beforehand in case our fight runs long."

Xenah's pointer finger twitched against the hilt of his sword. Though his back was turned to Tetsunah, and she lay at an angle in which she couldn't see his face, she knew his usual smirk had returned. "It won't be long."

"Sefah, no!" Kamari grabbed his arm and pulled him away. "If you fight Xen, you'll die. We can think of another way—a way that doesn't involve killing any of us!"

He carefully pried his arm free, pressing a kiss to her knuckles. "Maybe my death is the best way to end this," he whispered.

As his focus shifted to her, the stabbing cold in Tetsunah's veins lessened. The ice began to clear, little by little, easing the pressure in her lungs. Her pale skin was restored to its normal color, dusted red from the chill in the air—smooth as if completely untouched by frost. She drank in a greedy breath of air to fill the emptiness that choked her. Winter's grip on her began to fade as Sefah suspended the curse, readying to die with it or hand it over to Xen.

Tetsunah's vision turned watery. Though fading, ice still scraped her throat raw, and it stung with a burning pain. She wanted to argue, to tell Sefah his death was never the answer, but the words remained trapped in her mind. Frigid tears slid down her face, dripping onto the stone beneath her head. Sefah's blurry figure took his position across from Xen's blurred back, their swords raised. The cave was too small for a proper duel, but outside the snow would be too thick to fight in. Such a confined space would work in Xen's advantage, as everything would in this cruel arrangement. Sefah would die at Xen's hand; the vision of his body at her feet would soon come true.

Think, Tetsunah! Panic and fear gave her the shaky strength to right herself, arms trembling beneath her weight. Her cloak, now draped over her shoulders, pressed down on her with an unusual weight. Its gold embroidered edges glistened in the light from Xen's magic as he readied himself for the fight. She watched, counting the seconds until they would spring and tear each other to shreds. Her mind turned, spinning as she recalled Sefah's solutions. He couldn't wrangle winter himself in time, he couldn't call aid from the spirits without Deiah, and his third option was incomplete without a sacrifice. *Living being,* he had said. *It requires a single, living being, someone who possesses strong magic.*

Magic belonged to many creatures of the world, not simply humans, elves, and dragonborn. An idea sparked. Tetsunah perked up, swiping her bangs out of her face with trembling hands. "Living… being," she rasped. Her voice came out hoarse, scraped by the ice that had choked her throat raw, but she didn't care. Kamari swiveled her gaze to her and understanding formed between them. "He said… *living being.*"

It was too late. Xen lunged for Sefah with his sword raised. Sefah tensed, eyes narrowing as he focused on the movement. In an instant, he lifted his sword in time to block Xen's strike. A loud crack echoed through the air; Xen's blade split Sefah's, wedging itself into the icy sword. He jerked it free with ease, and Sefah stumbled forward, jaw clenched and left eye flashing. Sparks of blue danced at his fingertips as the threads of his magic returned. Xen took another swing at him, precise and swift. He danced out of the way, his arms tucked close to his body. As Xen turned, Sefah thrust his hand out, palm glowing blue, and—

"*Stop!*"

Kamari leapt between the two of them, arms outstretched to block their paths to one another. Her white cloak fluttered before settling gracefully around her, draping her in the blinding purity of the snow outside the cave. Her black curls and silver tinsel were striking against the fur-lined neck. A tight frown creased her lips and knitted her brows together. She stared unflinchingly back at Xen. He backed down, quickly resting a hand to his wounded side.

Sefah immediately dropped his hand and extinguished the glow, eyes wide as he studied her back. "Kamari, we have an agreement," he said. "You have to let us finish the duel."

"No." Tetsunah eased herself to her feet. The world rocked beneath her, vision flickering as a ringing flooded her ears. Her hand met the wall, and she took a moment to breathe until her vision cleared. When it did, she steadied herself and faced the three. "There's another way. Sefah, when you told me earlier that you could condense the wrath into a curse and place it inside a single being, I assumed you meant a *person*, but you never said that. A being could be any creature. So, what did you mean by that?"

He blinked. "Any being that holds strong enough power to feed the curse, so…" His eyes lit up and his back straightened. Laughter spilled from his lips, a wild grin replacing the heavy look that had lingered on his face for so long. "*Any* magical creature will do!"

Xen dispersed his sword into a shower of gold flecks. "You lost me."

Patting his arm as she passed, Tetsunah headed for the mouth of the cave. Outside, the storm raged on, raking the snow with windy claws and spitting hail on the land far below the overcast sky. Crisp mountain air flooded her lungs. It clouded in her face when she exhaled. "We're going to end the wrath of winter," she said, "and keep our family intact."

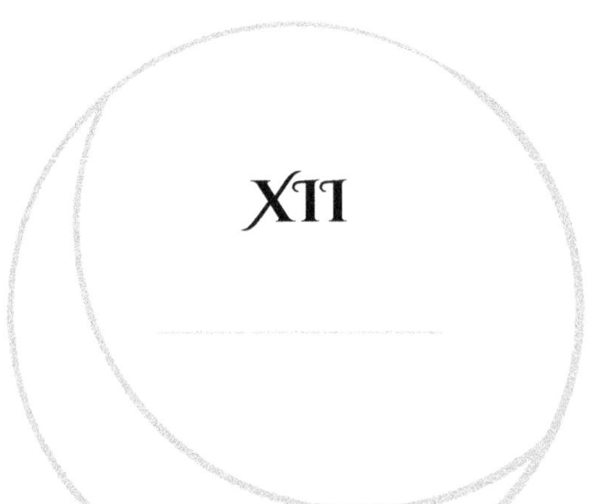

The idea of killing an innocent creature wriggled painfully under Tetsunah's skin, almost as cold as the ice that had nearly destroyed her. She knew what kind of pain they would be inflicting—after all, she suffered it herself for a mere moment. No matter how much she loved nature and the animals that took refuge in her season of spring, though, she could not place them above the lives of her people. However, this noble thought could only patch the cracks in her resolve, not completely mend them.

Together, the four left the small cave and descended back into the stormy Aurora Range. Since Tetsunah had taken on the curse for a few minutes, the strength of the wind seemed to have died down. Hail turned to heavy snowfall and the ominous dark clouds seemed less threatening than before. Or maybe it was because Sefah was with them now, his mind finally clear of winter's control. He was no longer a threat, but rather was their aide and the only one who could deliver the curse to the creature they chose.

"We need to find something before the sun goes down,"

Sefah said, shielding his eyes as he squinted at the dark sky. A frown darkened his features. "I can't say exactly how much time we have, but I'd guess a few hours."

"No need to fret. I'm an excellent hunter." Xen tucked his chin into his scarf as he scanned the snow-covered landscape. "I'll find us something."

Kamari wrapped herself in her cloak, shivering against the wind. It whipped through her hair and the string of blue jewels strung between her horns. "Should we split up and meet at the foot of the peak at dark?"

Something tightened in the pit of Tetsunah's stomach, and she tasted the fearful, bitter tang of bile on her tongue. Already, she could feel her idea beginning to break apart in the face of the task. She swallowed and licked her lips. "And if we haven't found anything by then?"

"Then we'll determine our next course of action after we gather together again." Sefah smiled softly, returning to the gentle, patient Sefah from her memories. "It's going to be okay. Xenah knows how to hunt and so does Kamari. We'll find something."

"I'll go with Tet," Xen announced as he snaked his arm around her shoulders and pulled her in close against his chest. "Catch, not kill, right?"

"Catch." Sefah nodded. "Kamari and I will head out to the northernmost valley. Be sure to be on your way back before—"

"I know, I know." Xen waved his hand and turned, pulling Tetsunah with him. Before she could say goodbye, he was already marching her away from Sefah and Kamari.

The crunch of snow occupied the silence that stretched between them. Tetsunah was simultaneously grateful for it and frustrated by the reminder of the chill that sank beneath her skin. She shivered and wrapped her arms around herself if only to keep some of her warmth in. However, they barely made it a few feet before Xen stopped dead in his tracks and whirled to face her, golden eyes blazing.

"What were you *thinking?*" he shouted as his strong grip closed tightly around her arms, shaking her. "Do you have any idea how reckless that was? Killing yourself to stop this?"

Tetsunah recoiled. "I thought it was the only way at the time."

"It wasn't, Tet!"

"I won't let you kill him!" she snapped, balling her fingers into a fist. She jerked free of his hold and glared back at him just as sharply. Frustration sprouted in the depths of her core, splitting her outward shell of calm like weeds breaking through cracks in stone. "That's no better than all the deaths caused by the uncontrolled winter. Mine was a willing sacrifice, Xen. I did it because you and everyone else deserve better." She paused as something different fluttered inside her—nervousness, regret, anxiety, pity... she couldn't tell which it was. She swallowed hard and swept her gaze over him.

His tan skin had paled, beaded with sweat from exerting his wound. Exhaustion hung over him like a heavy wet blanket. It was a miracle he was still standing at all.

Taking a deep breath, she released her anger and gently touched his arm. "I was okay with giving myself so that you could heal and live in peace. You're always there for me. I want to be there for you, too."

For the second time, tears welled in his eyes. He squeezed his eyes shut and crushed her in a hug, his arms wrapped firmly around her shoulders. The embrace was tight; she was squished against him, breathing in the sharp scent of pine that lingered in his scarf as she awkwardly snaked an arm around him.

"Don't ever do something like that again," he whispered, his voice wavering with the beginnings of a choked up sob. "I don't want to lose you, too—or Sefah. You're both more than fellow spirits to me. You know that, right?"

"Of course I do." Tetsunah squeezed him back. "You might consider telling Sefah though."

Xen snorted. "He can figure it out himself."

"It will be hard if you keep up this attitude."

"We should get going." Quick to dismiss her comments, he pulled back from the embrace, holding her at arm's length for a moment longer. She smiled up at him, and he returned the gesture with a shaky version of his usual grin. "Don't want to waste daylight," he said.

She nodded. "Lead the way."

Confidence sparked to life in his eyes and washed away all lines of exhaustion from his face. When he turned, shielding her from the wind with his form, her heart fluttered with excitement. Xen was skilled in this field. No snow nor foul weather would stop him. They would have their magical creature by day's end, and the wrath of winter would be stopped.

She crept forward behind him as he directed, body tense to keep her steps as silent as possible. Her steps weren't as silent as Xen's, but the crunch of snow beneath her boots was so soft that she was certain it would slip by unnoticed. Even her ears, blessed with sensitive hearing, had trouble picking out the sound. Though she wondered if it was the pounding of her heart against her ribs that drowned it out.

Before long, they made it back to the flat stretch of cliffs where Rym had left them. Snow blanketed the earth in a soft cushion of white. Their footsteps had been hidden away by fresh snowfall, swept clean as the storm raged on. Even the deep indentations from where Rym had sunk into the ground were gone. Xen paused, lips twitching down into a frown. Lifting a hand, he called upon the threads of his magic, brightening the golden aura around him as it sparked to life at the tips of his fingers. With the flick of his wrist, he dispersed a tiny ball of light. It floated lazily to the ground and drifted away from them.

Xen leaned toward Tetsunah and whispered in her ear,

"Tracks. If there's anything that has passed through this area recently, we'll be able to tell in no time."

"Will we know if it possesses enough magic to take on the curse?" she whispered back, already tasting something bitter at the thought.

"We'll find out."

She twisted the hem of her cloak. The ball of light swirled across the ground, inches from touching the snow. It moved slowly, free of the anxiety that ate away at the back of her mind. Magic held no fear of winter's wrath; it knew it would continue even if the world was destroyed.

With a bright flash, the light came to a stop. It circled something in the snow three times over before it wilted away.

Xen motioned for Tetsunah to stay. Slowly, he crept forward, head low and shoulders tense. As he approached, he knelt to examine the ground, ears pricked like a nervous animal. "Some kind of small dragon," he said. He dragged his hand across the snow and pointed farther out from the peak they had come from. "That way."

Aren't dragons nocturnal predators? Tetsunah gripped her cloak tighter, bunching it in her fist. "Will it be out at this time of day?"

"The cold forces them out of hiding more often during the day. A small one like this definitely won't be sleeping either. If we can track it back to its den, we have a shot of catching it." He kept his head bent, gaze locked on the tracks. He stayed that way a moment longer; Tetsunah could practically see his mind weighing the options behind the scenes. Finally, he stood and dusted the snow from his pants. He summoned another ball of light and flicked it along the path he had directed earlier. "It's worth a shot."

They followed the light down the dragon's trail, keeping close to the small prints left in the snow—though they were slightly larger than Tetsunah's foot, she couldn't help but think of them as tiny for a dragon. It was by no means as big as Rym, hinting that it was still quite young or perhaps a type that would not grow as large. She knew very little about which dragons would take up nesting in a place as unforgiving as the Aurora Range, but they seemed to be in abundance all over Anticuus. There was no place where Lady Selini and Lord Taiyo's dragons did not also reside. Like weeds, they could take root in the harshest of places without trouble.

Xen explained that he would take the lead and instructed Tetsunah to stay back and downwind so that the creature wouldn't catch her scent. She reminded him time and time again that they were sent only to capture it; he responded patiently every time, but she could see the twitch in his jaw that betrayed his unspoken thoughts. She clamped her mouth shut after that and hung back.

The stench of blood hit her long before the den came into sight. Crimson droplets mingled with the dragon's tracks, now combined with a deep etch in the snow where something was dragged through it. She wrinkled her nose and covered it with her cloak. "Is that a good sign?"

"This is the dragon's territory. It must have had a successful hunt." Xen swiped his hand and dispersed the light. Hunching forward, he prowled on. "Stay here," he said. "I'll draw it out. If it runs at you, catch it."

"Catch it?" she sputtered, twisting her cloak. "It's bound to be bigger than me, I—"

"You wanted this. You can help."

Swallowing hard, she nodded. Flecks of warm magic settled in the tips of her fingers, and she allowed it to bolster her confidence. She shifted her stance, determined and ready. No matter what sort of creature emerged from the nest, she would be ready and waiting for it.

Xen crawled toward a mound in the snow, steps light as a cat's. Lifting his hands, he wove a net from the gold threads of his magic. A sharp call fled his lips—it mimicked the cry of prey, Tetsunah noticed. As he crept closer, she stiffened, heart pounding. The wait was agonizing. Time was not something they could spare, and yet the little dragon didn't seem to care about the storm and the plague that threatened the world beyond the Aurora Range.

After a moment, a scaled snout poked out of the den, followed by the midnight blue head of the dragon. Its beady black eyes scanned the landscape, nose sniffing the air as it crawled out of the den. It was roughly the size of a large wolf with wide, taloned feet and pointed spines along its back that trailed down to the tip of its long tail. It had no wings, and its horns were barely longer than Tetsunah's finger. Blood was smeared across its lips, licked away by a forked tongue that shot out from behind its teeth. Magic circled the dragon in erratic, uneven waves—there was power in the creature, but it held no control over it. It was a low class dragon, one that was more like a wild animal than the revered beings of legend.

Once it was a few steps out of the snowy mound, Xen sprang in front of the den and threw the net. The dragon skittered out of the way with a hiss, baring its fangs. It turned sharply and dashed away from him, barreling straight for Tetsunah.

"Tet!" Xen summoned a bow and arrow with his magic and aimed for the dark blue creature. "Block it before it gets away!"

"Don't shoot!" she cried, leaping into the dragon's path. Panic snatched the breath from her lungs. Up close, its head came up past her waist, the black eyes locked on her swirling with malice.

The dragon was on her in seconds, teeth bared as it leapt into the air with a guttural roar. Xen's arrow speared its side. Thrown off course, it collapsed at her feet and choked out a snarl. Blood soaked the snow, oozing out from between its scales, but the beast heaved itself up again in a matter of seconds. This time, however, Xen's gold threads snagged its legs, tangling it in a net that burned with a fierce amber light. The dragon howled and squirmed, clawing wildly at the threads. Sparks flew, but the net remained intact.

Grinning, Xen closed his fingers into a fist, tightening the net around the wriggling dragon, and lifted it into the air. "Easy enough."

Tetsunah shot him a glare as she joined his side. The dragon hissed when she approached, eyes wide and fierce as they swung toward her. Her heart leapt to her throat, and she jerked back. "Xenah," she warned.

He dismissed the bow in his other hand. "It's still alive," he said with a shrug, as if he already knew what she was going to say. "Let's take it back."

She glared at him, nostrils flaring. "It's going to die before we get there." She gestured sharply at the blood-soaked snow beneath the net. "I can't heal it. My magic is still weak, remember?"

"It won't die." He waved his hand. "Take the arrow out, and it'll be fine. Does this thing look strong enough for Sefah's… spell?"

Gritting her teeth, Tetsunah turned to the caged dragon hovering between them. There was nothing to say. Only Sefah would know what was strong enough to contain winter's wrath and what wasn't. She could only focus on getting the dragon back alive—with as much of its strength as she could preserve. When she reached for the arrow through the yellow threads, it didn't fight. Gingerly, she took the arrow in both hands and snapped the fletching off. It broke into thousands of tiny gold sparks in her palm, scattered in the wind. The point of the arrow remained embedded in the dragon's side, squeezed by dark blue scales on either side. Her fingers brushed the smooth scales. With a snarl, the dragon twisted and snapped at her. Fear sparked in her core, and she jerked her hand away with a gasp. A growl rolled from the back of the creature's throat, lip curled to reveal a set of sharp teeth. Even in weakness, it warned her to stay away.

"It's a wild animal, Xen." She rubbed her hand absently. "It's not going to accept my help."

He sighed and raked his fingers through his cinnamon colored hair, the gold tips growing dull from use of magic. "Sorry. This will have to do."

The dragon squirmed against the netting again, its body twisted awkwardly in the confines of Xen's spell. Tetsunah's heart twisted with pity for it. "Can you carry it back with your magic?"

"I can try." He turned, guiding the net with him, and began to walk back to the peak. "Let's go. We should get there before dark."

THE WALK back to the foot of the peak took longer than leaving had. With his magic constantly at use containing the dragon and supporting his wounded body, Xen's steps soon began to slow, his confidence fading as his golden eyes grew dull. Each time the dragon thrashed, he winced, yanked off balance by its erratic movements. Tetsunah steadied him, chewing her lip as she eyed the angry beast. Despite the blood oozing from its side, it had yet to still. Its scales glowed with a pale light instead. *Perhaps it truly does hold enough magic to support Sefah's curse.*

"Tetsunah," Xen murmured. "I think…" He slumped forward, dropping unceremoniously into the thick snow, and the gold threads snapped as his control gave way.

"Xen!" Tetsunah's heart shuddered as she pulled him up. She pressed a hand to his cheek; warmth still clung to his skin, paired with the fog of his breath as he exhaled softly. She let out a sigh. He was exhausted, nothing more.

Behind her, the dragon's body fell into the snowdrift with

the soft crunch of ice. A low growl fled its lips, rolling easily from its throat. Tetsunah's relief shattered, and her skin prickled with unease. Cradling Xen close to her body, she shifted to face the unchained beast. Malice swirled in the depths of its gaze, a pool deep enough to drown her if she let it. It bared sharp teeth at her and lunged with a roar.

Her breath snagged, heart fluttering, and she thrust her hand out at the dragon. Heat surged through her chest down to the tips of her fingers, and a brilliant light flashed. The dragon slammed into something shimmering in the air around her—a barrier. It glistened with the pink aura of her magic, imprinted with the image of the flower and surrounded by a faint floral scent, but it wasn't wholly her own. Another's touch was mingled with her own, familiar and warm, a welcome embrace that clung to her shoulders.

Snarling, the dragon slammed against the barrier again, scraping its long talons against the magic shield to no avail. Sparks caught fire on its midnight scales. The creature shrieked and dove back into the snow, but the orange-red flames raged on, guided by an unseen hand. They danced along the dragon's spines, ignorant as it curled fearfully away from the heat. Nothing could disrupt the rhythm of the flame—not the cold, not the snow, not the ice. It clung to life and warmth, yet it did not eat away the flesh of its prey. It was a gentle touch, she realized, meant only to protect and distract.

Tears welled in Tetsunah's eyes, awe coiling in the pit of her stomach. *It couldn't be...* "Deiah!" she cried, turning her gaze to the last rays of sunlight that lit the sky in a brilliant crimson, burning away winter's dark clouds. Buried deep in the pocket of her cloak, the amulet hummed, warmed by the presence of the spirit. A hot breeze whisked past her cheek, threading invisible fingers through her hair. Deiah's form was gone, killed with her physical body, but she was never truly gone. She lived in the summer, in the sun, in the flame she loved.

Capture your prey, the voice of summer's spirit whispered. A presence brushed Tetsunah's hand and lifted it. *End winter's wrath and free our people of this curse.*

Determination blossomed inside her and drew from the deepest wells of power buried deep within her soul. Threads of magic tangled around her fingers, pulsing with the beat of her heart. She jerked her hand out and unleashed the threads on the writhing dragon. They shot out from her net and bound the beast—flaming scales and all. With the last of its strength robbed by the flames, the dragon fell still, beady eyes flicking around anxiously as its sides heaved for air. There was no submission in its gaze; the longer she stared down at the dragon, the more anger and fear took hold of its snarling face. She pulled the threads taut and quelled the rising aura of magic that spiked in the air around it.

Well done. The wind shifted and carried Deiah's presence away, snuffing out the flames with it. Cold settled over Tetsunah once more as the sun finally vanished behind the peaks.

"Tetsunah!"

Ears pricked, she angled her head in the direction of the call. Soon, Kamari's white-cloaked figure appeared out of the growing dark, a beacon that gleamed in the blackness. Sefah hurried at her side, his frost-covered hands glowing with a brilliant blue light and his snowy white hair hanging in his eyes. He reached her first, snow crunching heavily as he came to a stop. Worry creased his brow, and when his gaze hesitated on Xen's unconscious form, his breath hitched.

Tetsunah pulled on the threads. "We managed to catch something. Will this work?"

"Huh?" Sefah jolted to attention and swung to face the captured creature sprawled in the snowdrift. His shoulders stiffened as if he had only just now noticed it—and perhaps he had, due to his poor eyesight. "Yes. Yes, this is a mountain drake. It has quite the powerful aura. How did you—?"

One pink thread snapped. Tetsunah winced. Already, her strength was ebbing away and turning her limbs to lead. "I can't hold it forever. It's aggressive."

"Of course." He turned sharply, hand outstretched to the dragon.

Its eyes went wide, and its lips fell slack. All aggression fled its body, now turning to trembling in the face of winter's master. With a whimper, it shrank away from his ice-touched fingers, but it was too late. At the barest brush with Sefah's skin, the curse spread through the drake's body, freezing over its skin in delicate swirls of frost. Ice quickly claimed it.

Pity snagged Tetsunah's heart like sharp claws. Biting her lip, she jerked her face away, her chest painfully tight as if squeezed by thorny roots. Gradually, her hold on the magic slipped and the threads dispersed. There was no need for such a cage anymore. The creature had nowhere to run.

Kamari knelt beside Xen, her touch gentle for once as she checked for breathing. The tension fled her shoulders as she sighed in relief. "He'll wake soon," she said, turning to Tetsunah with a faint smile. "Used up all his magic, huh?"

Tetsunah gave a soft chuckle. "You know him. Stubborn to the end."

Kamari dipped her head in a nod, black curls concealing the look on her face. "That Xen," she muttered. "It seems we can't take him anywhere."

"I'm still here you know," Xen argued. Though there was bite in his words, his voice came out as barely more than a whisper. He scrunched his face but didn't open his eyes. "By the way... where's *your* animal, Kamari?"

She gave a snort and lifted her chin, jewels clinking against her silver horns. "Our hunt was cut short. We saw that light and thought something must have happened to you. You're lucky we came when we did."

Xen's retort fell on deaf ears. Tetsunah left them to their usual bickering to rejoin Sefah. He stood watch over the dragon, stiff as a statue. Sadness darkened his bright blue eyes, and when she approached, he looked away and pinched his lips into a thin line. Starlight painted him in a silver glow. The cover of dark clouds had already begun to thin, opening the world to the night sky once more.

"It was Dei, wasn't it?" Sefah asked, the first to break the silence for once. "She came to help you and called me and Kamari here."

Tetsunah nodded slowly, her tongue too heavy to form the words. A light so brilliant, drenched in red-orange like a fire, could only come from the spirit of summer herself.

"I feel as though I am being tested," he murmured. His pointed ears twitched and folded down slightly, a thoughtful frown taking shape on his lips. "I was nothing more than prey to my whims—to the power I was given to *control*." He scoffed. "Was it always so simple?"

Tetsunah looked down at the aching snowflake shaped scar on her palm and rubbed her thumb over the rough skin. "You… never thought to try this method before?"

"I was too weak to break winter's control on my own. I could do nothing but watch as I tore the world apart. That's why I can't waste any more time. Too much has been spent already." With a wry smile, he added, "I am blind in more ways than one, it seems. Deiah was always right about that."

Tetsunah cautiously stepped toward the dragon—or drake, as Sefah had called it—and, when it didn't fight, sank to the ground beside it, folding her legs beneath her. Its nostrils flared, eyes wide and never still. Despite the cold that rolled off it, the drake didn't shiver. It remained perfectly still as if sculpted from the ice that hardened on its body. Time was short for the creature, and the wrath of winter would soon come to an end. Tetsunah stroked its head in calm, soothing motions. Tears blurred her vision; she blinked them away furiously. *It's just an animal. It's not a person.*

It stilled, nose no longer twitching and eyes growing distant and empty. The color drained from its brilliant scales as the magic fled its body. Ice consumed it from the inside out. As the life was snuffed from its body, so was the curse of winter.

Sefah surveyed the sky as the last of the clouds dispersed. When he turned to face her again, the white glow in his eyes had disappeared entirely. Finally, the beast was quelled, silenced by the master's control. A shaky smile rose to his face. "The frostbite plague should fade as well. Venni and everyone else will heal. However, anyone that has already fallen…" He swallowed and dropped his fists to his side. "I can do nothing for the dead."

Those that he *killed.* The words were left unspoken, but Tetsunah knew they echoed in the minds of everyone present. Too many had died already, all because of the choices—the fear and loss of control—of one. Tetsunah chewed her lip and dipped her head down. The drake that lay still in the snow, consumed by the ice like so many people she had failed to help along the way, was the final life he would have to take because of the nightmare. The final victim of winter's wrath.

Kamari reached for Sefah's hand, brushing his ring with her thumb as she locked her fingers with his. She kissed his knuckles—his attention snapping back to her at the motion. When he looked at her, she offered a smile. "Let's get you home."

"I don't deserve this power," he said in a broken undertone. Shaking his head, he added, "I don't deserve to come home."

"Of course you do." Kamari cupped his cheek. His eyes fluttered shut as he leaned into her touch. "You can always come home," she said. "We can work through this together."

"What am I supposed to tell Venni? And Koen? Sara?"

"The truth probably." Xen righted himself slowly with a wince and crossed his arms with a sniff. "You'll tell everyone the truth, and we will all work hard to make sure this never happens again."

"If it does, Xen will know to bring you an offering instead of trying to tear your throat out." Kamari grinned at Xen, a mocking gleam in her pale blue eyes.

He tucked his chin into his scarf. "I don't want to talk about it," he grumbled.

Her usual self restored, Kamari exchanged another witty blow with Xen, who always answered in turn. Tetsunah let their conversation drown into unintelligible noise at the back of her mind as she knelt and began to scoop back the snow. Her fingers burned with cold, numb from spending hours at its mercy. When the hole was deep enough, she began to push the frozen body of the drake inside. It barely moved an inch until Sefah came over to help. Together, they buried it beneath the snow. It felt foolish that the answer lay in something so small, that so many had suffered because of Sefah's blindness.

Without Deiah's light, it seems we were all trapped in the dark. With that hanging over her, she stood. "I need to return to Aire to help with the recovery. Xen?"

"I'll go with you. You're no doubt still recovering yourself." Smiling, he took her outstretched hand and squeezed. A touch of light returned to his eyes, brightening the gold that swirled in their depths. "Rym will be here in no time."

His confidence was contagious, though she didn't understand how it could return so quickly. Tetsunah smiled back before she even had a chance to consider why she was doing it. Hope surged through her, bright and unwavering for the first time in months. It made her body strangely light, her shoulders finally freed from some invisible weight. Yes, there was reason to celebrate. Her people were saved, the storm was cleared, Sefah was found. She couldn't spend her life choking on regret.

For now, she would face the light with her head high and leave the darkness behind.

"Sefah?" she asked, questing toward him. "What have you decided?"

Though the shadow on his face had not yet lifted—persistent despite the mood that lifted the rest of them—he nodded to her. "It is time that I return home."

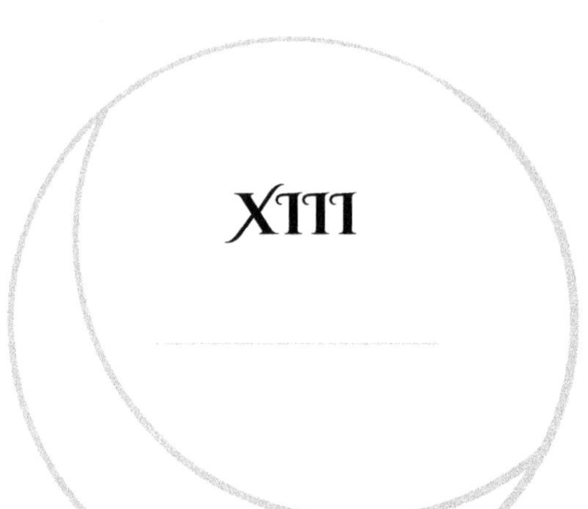

XIII

Rym landed in the outskirts of Aire, wings fluttering back in against his sides as his talons touched the ground. Evening rays of sunlight bathed him in a pleasant glow, the pink and orange of the sunset reflected in his shimmering scales. He hummed cheerfully and stretched his neck, eyes closed. Tetsunah giggled and gave his shoulder a quick pat before she slid down. Green grass rose beneath her boots, quickly overtaking the dead, brown weeds left behind by the winter storm. A cool breeze kissed her cheek, combing the pink tips of her hair. It was a refreshing break from the steady warmth of Rym's scales and the unforgiving chill of winter's wrath. Instead, it was a gentle reminder of spring.

"Tetsunah!"

She spun toward the voice just as Erix's figure appeared around the corner of a small stable house at the edge of town. Her vision turned watery, and her breath snagged in her throat. He ran toward her with open arms, a wide grin on his face. In mere seconds, he crossed the distance between them and scooped her up. They both laughed as he spun her around before setting her back on her feet, his arms wrapped around her waist. He touched his forehead to hers, his gaze soft as he studied her face.

"Your skin." She pulled back with a gasp, cupping his face in her hands. The scar on his forehead had faded to nothing but a small scratch, pale against his skin. There was no blueness in his ears nor his fingers. No ice or frost eating away at his body.

"It's gone." He grinned and rested his hand against hers. "Everyone is healing. The plague has completely disappeared. You did it, Tetsunah."

For a moment, words completely fled Tetsunah's mind. It took all her energy to keep from crying again, despite that it was laughter which burst from her lips as she folded into Erix's embrace. A fresh wave of relief coursed through her, washing clean the sands of fear that itched beneath her skin for so long. "I'm glad you're okay," she finally said after a moment.

"Me too," he whispered. His fingers brushed her forehead, smoothing her bangs back from her face. They were warm, finally void of the plague's incessant cold. "I was worried when your magic fled."

My magic. She popped her head back up, snapping her gaze up to his brown eyes. "The others. Where are they? How is everyone doing?"

"They're still below ground. I went up to check things after I began to heal." He pulled back, hands entwining with hers. A barely perceptible smile cracked his calm mask. "Come see for yourself."

Xen cleared his throat loudly behind them. Tetsunah jumped. He stood beside Rym, arms crossed and one brow raised in a questioning stare as he glanced between the two of them. Her face warmed. In all the excitement, she had forgotten he had come with her.

"Lord Xenah!" Erix snapped his hand away from Tetsunah's and bent into a stiff, awkward bow. "It is an honor to have you

here with us. Forgive me. I did not realize you came with Te
—*Lady* Tetsunah."

"I can see that," Xen grumbled. With the roll of his eyes, he dropped his dark stare and waved his hand in a dismissive manner. "Don't mind me. Carry on. I'm just here to make sure Tetsunah made it back safely herself. I must return to Calistie City to see how the people are faring."

"Yes, of course. Please do not feel pressured to stay if you have business of your own to attend to."

"If Tetsunah will be in good hands here, I'll be going." He searched her face, one brow raised in question.

Tetsunah offered him a reassuring smile. Already her strength had returned, and she no longer felt the weakness in her knees that her brief contact with the icy curse had left behind. Even her magic was steadily returning, spurred on by spring's resurgence in the air itself.

"She will. I promise." Erix's fingers nudged hers again. The shy smile on his face set her heart fluttering.

Xen snorted, watching them. He shook his head, gold-tipped locks swaying. "Take care, Tet. You know where to find me if you need me. And… you did good today." With one last, lingering look—a glimmer of pride settling in the depths of his gaze—he turned and climbed onto Rym's back.

"Rest well, Xenah!" she called. He already seemed better than he had when they left the mountains, but his skin was still slightly pale, his eyes lacking their usual amber-gold glow. Even if he refused to admit it, he was the one that needed to be looked after, not her.

He said nothing, but she caught a flash of a smile, a promise that things would be alright.

The mighty sun dragon bowed to Tetsunah and Erix before bounding off toward the distant forests and taking to the sky in one big leap. Tetsunah waved until he shrank to barely a speck against the sunset sky.

"Come on." Erix tugged lightly on her arm again. "They're eager to see you."

She let him guide her away. Together, they raced back to the shielded entrance of the underground. It parted for their entrance, and they slipped inside, laughing to each other. Erix's hand squeezed hers, the touch full of comfort and security. With the fading light of the sun against her back and the touch of grass against her boots, Tetsunah felt right once again. Not even rounding the end of the tunnel to face the crowd of elves and humans awaiting her could disrupt the airiness of her mood.

This time, it wasn't a hoard of scowls and frightened, wide eyes that awaited her. The room wasn't thick with the cold air of the sickness or the ever-present caress of death just waiting to collect another soul. This time, when she entered the room, the people erupted into cheering and applause. It was deafening, echoing off the smooth walls of the underground and roaring in her ears. Startled, she stepped back, flattening her pointed—and rather sensitive—ears back. Erix's hand landed against her back to steady her.

"Lady Tetsunah!" A woman made her way to the front of the crowd, eyes rimmed with tears. Her pale skin was cleared of the icy veins that once split it like cracks in dry ground. Though her eyes were red and blotchy, it didn't possess the same cold-touched look as those who were sick. She clasped Tetsunah's hand firmly and bowed low before her. "Thank you, thank you. My son, he was healed. Thank you, goddess of spring."

Her son? Tetsunah's gaze dropped to the little boy trailing after her, the very same she had said would not make it more than a few days. Though shaky and weak, his face not yet restored to a healthy color, he too was free of winter's frigid touch. Tetsunah lifted the woman's head. "Please, I am no goddess, and I do not deserve your thanks." Raising her voice, she turned to address the rest of the crowd. "It was Sefah, the lord of winter, who lifted this curse from you all. If he hadn't, I too would have been claimed by it. He's the one you should thank."

"The storm has cleared," Erix said, stepping forward to join Tetsunah's side. He raised his voice to address everyone in the room. "You are free to return above ground. If anyone is still feeling weak or showing signs of the frostbite plague, please see myself, Tetsunah, or the other healers before you leave."

With one final, quick thank you, the woman and her son pulled away and began to file out with the rest of the crowd. Many bowed their heads as they passed, some stopping to murmur thanks. Tetsunah shifted awkwardly under their watchful stares. The attention was stifling.

Even so, she couldn't help but smile at each face that turned her way. The sickness was gone, the storm had cleared, and the people of Aire were finally free.

"I THOUGHT I might find you here." The murmur of Sefah's voice drifted to Tetsunah's ears, carried along by the dance of the fair spring breeze. His steps were light like a cat, barely making a sound against the soft, green grass as he approached.

Tetsunah raised her head and met the sight of his usual smile —just the tiniest upturned twitch at the corners of his mouth. The glow in his white snowflake rune had died down, allowing the blue of his eyes to shine through. Wind toyed with his white hair, half hidden beneath the wrap which hung over one side of his face. Amid the blossoming pink flowers and vibrant grass of her fields, he stood out painfully, like the Aurora Range mountains stood against the azure sky and loomed over the earth.

She patted the ground beside her, and he sat, kneeling among the white lilies. Weariness etched deep lines under his eyes, but the melancholy that had forced him to sit hunched over with his head low seemed to have left him.

"I went through the town looking for you," he said. "Everyone looks well. Are they fully healed now?"

"For the most part. There are a few elderly humans that Erix is keeping watch over. All the elves have made swift recoveries. It's amazing what a few weeks can do." The town itself was almost fully restored as well. The holes punctured by the hail had been quickly patched up after her return, and the ground responded eagerly to her power as she eased it back to life. It wasn't long before the scar left behind by winter's wrath had faded completely.

Sefah picked at the grass, plucking it from the dirt and twirling it between his dark, frost-coated fingers. "They thanked me, you know. Nearly everyone I passed stopped to thank me. They've... never done that before." He split the grass between his fingers and dropped his hands with a sigh, turning his gaze to Tetsunah. "I don't deserve that, Tet. I'm the one that cursed them. I'm that one that unleashed that storm, I'm the one that sent the plague that took the lives of so many, and yet they're thanking me?"

"I told them you were the one that freed them," she murmured, tucking a stray strand of hair behind her ear. At his incredulous look, she added, "Don't argue. It's true. The only one who could control winter is you. They wouldn't be here if you hadn't come back to yourself and broken the spell."

"But—"

"I didn't do anything except help you see the light, Sefah." She pinned him with a serious look, lips pinched in a thin line. "*You* made the choice to right your wrong."

In the sunlight, the cool tones of his bronze skin seemed fainter, warmer. The silver needlework in his light blue tunic glittered in the light. Among the multitude of colorful flowers, bathed in the bright light, he seemed more ethereal, as if he came from a different plane altogether. Brow creased, he looked away.

"I'm sorry." He dragged a hand across his face. "I fear I can never say that enough times to make up for what I did."

"I know," she said, patting his knee. "Things will get better. Remember that Kamari, Xen, and I will always be by your side. Even Deiah is never truly far from us, right?" She paused, frowning. "How's... Venni?"

"She made a swift recovery and quickly returned to her normal self." He split another blade of grass. "She talks like Xen, you know. She looks up to him."

"He's close with her. I... didn't expect to be able to talk sense back into him after she came up sick."

Pursing his lips, Sefah plucked another blade of grass. "I spoke with the Being."

Tetsunah blinked, puzzled by his brash statement. The Being hadn't spoken to any of them since he had created them; she wasn't sure she even knew how to reach out to him if she wanted to. She tilted her head back and pondered his words. "It is good to pray," she finally said. It was the only thing that made sense to her.

"I asked him to remove my power," he muttered.

"Sefah—"

"He said no." Shaking the grass from his fingers, he traced the image of the snowflake rune through the air in front of them. A glowing thread of azure followed the tip of his fingers and solidified the rune. It hung between them, pulsing with the steady beat of his heart. "I cannot be Sefah without winter; it is part of me, and I am part of it. That's how it always will be. Part of me did give in to the wrath. That's why it was able to slip from my control in the first place." He sighed and dropped his hand back into his lap. The rune dissipated. "I saw war and felt pained by the future. All I wanted was a way to stop it. That turned to desperation, then fear, then anger, then I couldn't find my way back. If it was a test, I failed, and yet I remain the lord of winter. I don't *want* to be the winter spirit that people fear. I'm glad you were able to bring me home."

"Of course." She nudged his shoulder with her own. "You've done so much for me; it was my turn to give back to you."

He chuckled. "Settling debts is all that was, huh?"

"You know me better than that."

For a moment, they were content to sit in silence with each other. Sefah shifted, the first to break it as he smoothed his tunic down. "The Being said the wrath of winter will come again," he said. "If war is to come, I have no doubt of that."

The endless blue sky stretched overhead, dotted with fluffy, white clouds that drifted lazily across the expanse. *Peace*, it seemed to whisper, but peace could be such a fragile thing. Sefah's vision hung like a shadow over her mind, threaded with uncertainty. It poised like a knife over the delicate cloth of peace, ready to tear it apart as soon as the time was right.

Her gaze hardened, pink flecks of magic swirling around her fingers. Flowers bloomed beneath her hand, their petals soft as they skimmed the surface of her skin. As the spirit of spring, she had a duty to uphold balance and protect her people. If Selini wished to threaten her, she would be ready and waiting. Whatever the dragon queen sent their way, the people of Calistie would not fall.

She turned to Sefah again and held his gaze. "No matter what the future brings, we will stand with you," she finished.

His eyes darkened, lit by the fires of determination. He gave only a subtle nod, but she knew he understood the meaning behind her words.

The next time the wrath of winter was unleashed, it would be on Selini herself and her alone.

"Thus the lord of winter has spoken—a warning to all who would oppose him: his wrath is not yet quelled. It will rise again when the time is right and Selini will be destroyed. This is the promise he makes to the Kingdom of Calistie."

— THE HISTORY OF CALISTIE, VOL. III

ALSO BY ROBIN WINCKLER

The Legends of Anticuus series

The Wrath of Winter

Of Spellbooks and Thieves

Of Scars and Scales

Of Ice and Shadows - coming soon!

~

If you enjoyed this book, please consider leaving a review on Amazon.
They help more than you know!

Acknowledgments

The Wrath of Winter started as a tiny sliver of an idea—mostly a joke I had with friends that I could make yet another novella about untold lore in the world of Anticuus. I told myself I wouldn't write it because it didn't need to be told, even though it has ties to events later in the series. I thought it was better as a distant dream, a chunk of worldbuilding told through exposition or dialogue exchanged in other books. I was wrong, of course.

On February 1st of 2023, my school closed for the day due to icy weather. How could I pass up such a perfect opportunity to write when I had a shiny new idea? It was freezing outside, I was free of homework and classes, and I was in need of a break from my other projects. It was *perfect.* So I made myself a nice cup of hot cocoa, got comfy under a warm blanket, and wrote the day away. Thus, *The Wrath of Winter* was born. Sometimes it's good to write what you feel like writing, even if you don't believe anyone will want to read it. You may just prove yourself wrong.

Well, now that we have the history—the lore, if you will—of this branch of the Anticuus series out of the way, there are a few people I would like to thank for coming along this crazy ride.

Thank you to my parents for listening to me ramble about this crazy business plan I had to publish a short prequel novella before releasing book two because I was being admittedly a little slow with writing it. I'm consistently blown away by your love and encouragement. I hope I can continue to make you proud.

To my friends, readers, and critique partners: Thank you for giving this story your time, attention, and love! I couldn't have made it this far without each and every one of you, and I'm truly grateful for your support!

To Emma, for being Sefah's biggest fan even when he was making big mistakes and for providing feedback on just about every draft I threw at you. Your keyboard smashes and crying emojis kept me going on days when it was hard to write. To Sabrina, for making sure I always knew when what I was writing didn't make sense even if it vibed. And also for making sure Xen got some love—though I didn't always think he should. To Nicole, for encouraging me to draw lots of pretty pictures for this book and also for your crazy theories. Seriously, where do some of those ideas even come from? And to many others who supported this story while it was in the works. The list would go on forever if I were to name all of you and I would surely begin to run out of jokes, and we can't have that.

To my editors, Laine and Aria, who have a gift for finding all the errors I tried to ignore or didn't even know were there. I'm grateful for your help in turning this story into the best it can be. Thank you for your encouragement and excitement!

And finally, to YOU for reading! Thanks for coming with me on this journey!

ABOUT THE AUTHOR

Robin Winckler is a YA fantasy author with a love for magic, dragons, adventure, and all things high fantasy. She is currently pursuing a degree in English, which she hopes to use to grow her writing skills. When she is not writing, she can be found drawing, reading, or playing with her beloved dog, Pippin.

instagram.com/author.robinwinckler
patreon.com/authorrobinwinckler